In the deep it doesn't matter how loud you *scream*

THE *Dirty Heroes* COLLECTION

CRUEL
WATER

DEE PALMER

The Black Fox, by Brianna Hale

Finding His Strength, by Measha Stone

While She Sleeps, by Dani René

Bound by Sacrifice, by Murphy Wallace

Never Lost, by TL Mayhew

The Curse Behind The Mask, by Holly J. Gill

Clockwork Stalker, by Cari Silverwood

Kiss and Tell, by Jo-Anne Joseph

Skeleton King, by Charity B.

Make Me Real, by Petra J. Knox

Cruel Water, by Dee Palmer

The Masked Prince, by Faith Ryan

Hunted, by Cassandra Faye

The Lady, by Golden Angel

Once upon a time, a scorned Queen opened a box, unleashing horrible evil on the world's heroes.

Instead of gallantry and chivalry, they now possessed much more perverse traits. They've fallen victim to their darkest and most deviant desires.

This is one of their stories...

Cruel Water

I'm not a sadist by choice,
I'm a sadist by design,
Cursed to inflict pain on others
And yet I find no pleasure in it,
Only a moment of release from my eternal torment.
And yet, it's not enough
I'm not a sadist,
I'm a monster.

One night changed all that,
One night she dragged me from the oceans dark depths
Cresting the cruel waters she came to my rescue, like an
angel.
A mermaid.
And now I'm going crazy and don't know what to
believe.
Was she real?
Did she truly soothe my demons and take away my
pain?
How am I even alive?
So many questions taunt me.
So many answer evade my grasp.
What is true? What is real? What to believe?
All I know for sure is I have to find her again,
I have to know,
Can she really save me from myself?

CHAPTER
One

M Y NECK CRACKS WITH THE STRETCH, TENSION in the muscles of my shoulders, back, and everywhere else evaporating into the dimly lit room that now reeks of satisfied lust and broken spirit. Drawing in a satisfied breath slowly through my nostrils, I step back and survey my most recent masterpiece.

There's something so very beautiful about a face contorted with pain—raw, vulnerable and utterly truthful. They will clench their jaws, pinch their lips tight to prevent the howl of agony escaping, squeeze their eyes so tight in a valiant effort to take themselves anywhere other than here, with me. *This is their truth in the face of their lies.*

They tell me they want this. They crave the pain I offer, beg me, and each one has been so utterly convincing—right up to the point where their bodies tell a different story that allows them into my dark world. Cries muffled by the rubber gag in their mouth, as they stoically endure what I so desperately need to deliver. Shock will widen their eyelids. Desire might darken their pupils for a moment before it's too much, so much so that their eyes look like inky wells of hopelessness. Held breath and taut muscles are evidence of their level of endurance. Telltale twitches of parts of the body one would least expect reveal so much more than a desperate cry, but it's in the eyes I see their truth. They might be self-confessed masochists, because I insist that they are, still this is not fun. This is beyond; this is something they do because…

Because I'm broken, I'm a challenge, and they think if they give me what I want, they'll fix me. That I'll change maybe, that I'll be able to love. *They are so very*, very *wrong*.

I'm not broken; I'm cursed. As much as I might try to navigate around the proclivities of my predicament, I am left with the undeniable truth. I inflict pain because I need it. I need it to calm the demons in my soul, to quiet the storm that rages constantly in my head and catch a moment of peace. A sadist by design, not by nature, yet I can't deny how utterly captivating it is to witness someone giving themselves to me, completely.

It's intoxicating, and I've long since given up any hope of my life being any different. All I can do is manage my expectations and theirs.

"Would you like some water?" I ask. I'm not a complete monster. Aftercare is something I don't enjoy, but I know it's necessary. She nods, her face wet with tears, cheeks flushed a deep red hue, almost the same as the blood smeared across her breasts. She was very brave; I have to give her that. She blinks, and fat tears drop onto my knuckles as I place the glass against her bottom lip, the gag unclipped and now balanced on her neck like some sort of kinky novelty necktie.

Her body is stretched taut against the St. Andrews cross in my own private dungeon. It's frivolous to have a room just for my pleasure, I know, but it's my club, and I make the rules.

Rule one: I don't share.

Rule two: Actually, there aren't many rules after rule one. No that's a lie. There is one rule significantly more important than the no share rule; it's the 'L' rule. *Never speak, utter or even think the L word.*

She blinks again, sucking down large gulps of water. Her nostrils flare with the continued need to fill her lungs with fresh air. Her chest rises and falls with each labored breath. Her firm, round breasts swell and glow with the slick sheen of perspiration coating them. Blazing across her body like a Jackson Pollock painting, her once pale skin is littered with an intricate pattern of stripes, slashes, and the mottled hues of burgeoning bruises.

It's glorious.

I deftly unhook the restraints, and she falls limply against my naked chest. I tense. Not with her weight but with the soft sigh she releases and the tightness of her arms secured around my neck when I lift her in my arms. She winces when I move, and pain clearly flashes through her when I lay her carefully on the bed.

"Can I get you anything else?" The icy chill of indifference races the length of my spine, and I find myself straightening to full height, towering over her. Her response is innate; she shudders with a mix or worry and trepidation.

"No, no I'm fine. That was wonderful. Thank you, Sir." She lying, and I let out a heavy sigh. She swallows thickly and reaches for my hand; the glance I cast makes her recoil. She's right to be scared. I have no limits when it comes to inflicting pain. Still, even *I* have to draw the line somewhere. With all the tools in my arsenal, it's my honesty that always hurts the most.

"Then you are dismissed. Permanently." My level tone is implacable.

"What?" Her body curls around the impact. Her hand clutches to her chest as she lurches to sit up, swinging her legs over the edge of the bed. However, she doesn't try to stand, opting instead to pull her legs against her body to hug for comfort.

"You may remain a member of the club; however, if you approach me or attempt to contact me in any way, you will find your membership canceled."

"I...I don't understand. I did everything you asked. I took...I took everything. Why are you doing this?"

"Because I can." Dispassionate and without a hint of conflict, I deliver the final blow.

"You're so cruel." She sobs.

"Life's cruel." It's not a speculation; it's a fact. *Why should playtime be any different?*

"Please don't, Eric. Please let me in. I can help. If you'd just let me, please. I...I—" She stutters and I cut in.

"You what?" My lips curl around the sardonic snarl.

"Nothing." She sucks back the emotion, making her lips tremble. She bites them closed and lowers her head in resignation.

I get a twinge of something, regret maybe. Not of my decision, that was inevitable. I can't change who I am, and I won't let them believe otherwise. So maybe it isn't regret, maybe it's despair that what I am searching for simply does not exist.

"Good girl." I tuck her damp hair behind her ear and immediately regret the tender display of affection when her eyes glisten with fresh tears and misplaced hope. She worries her bottom lip, swollen from biting back the pain for the last hour. Before she can muster the courage to beg once more, I turn my back and walk out of the door.

That twinge wasn't regret. It wasn't guilt. It was self-loathing.

It would appear I am a monster, after all.

CHAPTER
Two

SLIDING A FRESH WHITE SHIRT ACROSS MY shoulders, I start to button up. The soft cotton clings to the residual dampness on my skin from my shower. I finish the last button when the door to my office bursts open and a fiery, raven-haired force of nature storms in, slamming the door behind her. I barely raise a brow, even if she's dicing with death by barging into my office with so little respect. If she wasn't such a good friend and an amazing manager, her flagrant disregard for my boundaries would be an issue.

As if the dramatic entrance isn't enough to indicate her current mood, she halts at the other side of my desk with a fierce scowl, narrow eyes, and her fists pressed hard against the smooth line of her tan leather pencil skirt. Her emerald silk blouse nips at her waist and is conservatively fastened over her ample breasts right up to her slender neck.

"What the fuck is wrong with you?" She is the epitome of calm and controlled. Even now, when her blood is clearly boiling, her voice maintains a level of threat with an undertone of menace that most Dominants would give their eyeteeth for.

"I take it that's a rhetorical question?" Slumping into my chair, I hope my bored indifference will be enough to end what I can only assume is going to be some sort of lecture. Kicking my legs up to rest my feet on the corner of my desk, I recline my chair to almost horizontal and tuck my hands behind my head. Stephanie growls and presses her fingertips pointedly on to the surface of my desk. Leaning over, the waves of frustration rolling off her force me to engage. There's a ridiculous silent standoff that I will take no pleasure in winning, even if I did have the energy.

Exhaling, I pull myself to sitting. Stephanie pours two tumblers of whiskey from the decanter on my desk and hands me one. She perches her curves on the desk and holds the glass up for me to clink. I'm not in the mood. I down the liquor and relish the blissful moment of burn hitting the back of my throat. She tops my glass up. Her features soften as she does. Her hazel eyes seem more feline than human with the way she applies her liner. Her lips are red and glossy. She is a very attractive woman, a timeless beauty, always immaculate, and only when this close, can one see the telltale soft lines around her mouth and the corners of her eyes that betray her age. Her tone, however, is still markedly pissed.

"No. No, it's not rhetorical. I seriously want to know what the hell, Eric! Why did you just end it with Belle? She was perfect." Her exasperation makes me bristle. It's not like I plan these things. It's not me that lies.

"She wasn't a true masochist, Stephanie."

"You ask too much, Eric. No one can endure *that* level of pain without getting *anything* back."

"I know." Tension pulses through the veins in my temples and crawls backward into the muscles in my neck. Stretching from one side and then the other, I try and ease the buildup. My fingers press hard against the pressure points, and when that doesn't work, I take another pull from my whiskey. My gaze meets Stephanie's. I can see she's waiting for more of an explanation, only I'm not sure I am inclined to share my own personal hell this early in the evening.

She lets out a heavy breath and tilts her head, her tone bordering on sympathetic. "You're the worst kind of sadist."

I scoff. "There's a good kind?"

"Yes, *I'm* the good kind. I love dishing out pain, humiliation, degradation as much as the next sadist, but I *love* my pain sluts. I adore that they give so much for my pleasure. You? You seem to despise them for it."

"I don't despise them, Stephanie. I *nothing* them."

"See, the worst. It's lucky I love you," she quips

"It's lucky I know you don't."

"Whatever. I care, and I hate seeing you like this." She moves to take the seat in the high backed leather chair opposite, though still close enough to continue as drink dispenser.

"Like what?"

"Lost. In pain. Alone. Take your pick." She pours some more whiskey. The uncharacteristic draw of her bottom lip into her mouth is evidence she is weighing how far she wants to take this conversation. I like her. She is probably the closest thing I have to a 'friend'; however, I don't do touchy feely bullshit. I keep my dark close and my demons closer. "You need to let someone in, Eric." I narrow my eyes, and she braces, her mouth tight and her shoulders straight.

"I need the release. That's *all* I need. That is the beginning, the middle, and the end of it. The difference between us," I clarify, "is I don't want to be like this. It's not a choice for me, and seeing them look at me like they can save me… Trust me, I'm doing her a favor." Rolling the tumbler around so the golden liquid coats the sides, the clear shine of the sugars clings to the glass before once more being swept into the swirling contents.

"She gave you the look, hmm?" Stephanie's insightful deduction is accurate as always. Reaching for my forearm, she squeezes.

I nod. "Yes. How can anyone look at me like that? With awe, longing, with *love*." The taste of that word in my mouth makes me want to retch. "They look at me like I'm some sort of god."

"Well, not to state the bloody obvious, but have you seen you recently? Six foot seven, muscles like Apollo, golden brown eyes that would set most panties on fire. And you do yourself no favors with the smoldering tortured soul routine. And cut your damn hair!" she tuts playfully; however, with my darkening mood, her attempt at humor is lost on me.

"I don't believe that."

"No, you're right. It's not just that. Looks will only get you so far in this game. But in here, you take them to a place few can understand, let alone appreciate. You say they are not true masochists. Well, you're wrong; they are. But even a good masochist can't exist in a vacuum. You have to give them something of yourself. They don't need rings and roses, just some acknowledgment that you see them, want them…need them. You are the Dominant, yes, but you are nothing without them."

"I know." Placing the glass down, I drop my head in my hands, feeling every bit of the weight of my darkness on my shoulders.

"You are the sorriest sadist I've ever met; that's for sure." She ruffles my hair and gives it a sharp tug so I am now looking at her earnest and somewhat troubled face.

"So now I'm a shit sadist?"

She sighs softly, and her red lips curve in

a motherly smile. "Eric you are… I don't know what you are." She shakes her head, and I feel her loss for words like a knife's point pressed to the throbbing vein in my neck.

"I'm cursed," I state coldly.

"How so?" Releasing her hold, her hand flies back as if I've said the most ridiculous thing since Zuckerberg said, 'of course your data's safe', and it's actually scalded her skin. "Cursed because you can't get aroused unless you are inflicting pain? Join the club. Oh wait… you already own it." Derision drips from her perfectly pursed lips, but the cut of her tone is dulled by the sympathetic tilt of her head.

"Cute," I snark, and reach once more for the decanter. She beats me to it and refills both our glasses. The alcohol is barely registering, and I've consumed almost half a bottle in this short time. I should be three sheets to the wind, yet I feel empty, numb, and not remotely drunk. I let out a heavy sigh and pinch the throbbing pressure at the bridge of my nose. The malty liquid rolls in my mouth before I swallow down another mouthful and face her. "If that was true, it wouldn't be so bad. I don't get aroused. I get a moment of respite from the constant torment, a moment of calm, but there is nothing sexual.

I wish there were. I wish I felt something other than this emptiness."

Her eyes widen and she gapes. It would be comical if this whole situation weren't so hopeless. "You don't ever get turned on?"

I shake my head.

"Not even when they are panting, glowing, floating in subspace because *you've* taken them to the edge of their boundaries and beyond?" Her pupils dilate simply from her own description, and I can't help the swirl of jealously in my gut. *If only.*

"No, nothing."

"But you can get hard?"

"Are we having this conversation?"

"I'm intrigued." She arches a brow, and as much as I don't wish to air my sticky laundry, I also don't need this conversation to become more than it is.

"Yes, I can get hard. Yes, I can come. And yes, I masturbate like a fucking monkey, but no woman—or man—has ever given me sexual pleasure. I get pleasure from pain. No, that's not entirely true. I get a different kind of pleasure from pain, and that gives me respite."

"So why do you think that is?" She slumps back in the padded high-back sumptuous chair, looking suitably perplexed. I'll take perplexed over sympathetic any day.

"I don't know. All I know is I need their pain to survive, and unless they love it, *truly* love it, without wanting more from me, well, I won't inflict my demons on someone who is misguided enough to believe I can change."

"Why is it so important to you? Can't you just pretend? After all, they aren't complaining."

"No!" I snap. Exhaling a deep and pained breath, I try and explain the unexplainable. "No pretense. I have to have some hope, Stephanie. Hope is all I have, *hope* that if I can find someone where the pleasure is *real*…then, it might just…"

"What? Might what?"

"It might break the spell and I might be able to feel desire, I might be able to have some peace without needing the pain of an innocent. I might not need the pain at all."

"Oooor the spell might be broken, and you find you are just as kinky as the rest of us and fucking love the pain."

"That would work also." I sniff, and a flat laugh slips from my mouth.

"Don't give me that. I know you love it. You can try the tortured soul routine on me, but I'm not buying it." Her second attempt to lift my mood is equally unsuccessful as the first. *I only wish that was the case.* She draws in a resigned and somewhat bored breath. "So you need to find someone that is basically mute, devoid of emotional needs, with nonexistent nerve endings?"

"Yes." I meet her gaze, her eyebrow raised high with cynical judgment.

"You're going to die a very lonely man, Eric," she quips, sad amusement pulling her lips in a downward arc.

"I know." My flat response makes her wince.

"Oh god, Eric, you may be a massive asshole, but I hate seeing you like this. I mean you've always been… a bit odd, but this? This is different. Ever since the accident last week. I don't get it, you'd think cheating death like you did would give you a fresh zest for life."

"I didn't cheat death, Stephanie, I was saved." My jaw twitches with fresh tension. A whole other can of worms is about to explode onto my desk, and I curse myself that I'm engaging.

"So you say, even after a massive concussion," she mutters.

My fist clenches around the tumbler and I jerk it up and slam it down. "Don't fucking do that! I know what happened. I saw what I saw!"

"Eric, you were unconscious." Holding her palms up in supplication, her voice takes on a softer tone, as if that will calm the inferno this conversation had ignited in my belly.

"Exactly. My car tore through the barrier as if it was tissue paper and hit the ocean like a fucking expensive stone. I don't remember trying to escape. I don't remember struggling at all."

"You must have passed out when you hit the barrier. Your body shut down. I heard that happens sometimes when the brain is faced with a life and death situation. It's a self-preservation thing."

Blinking slowly and with enormous effort, I try to block out what she's saying and pull the events back to the forefront of my mind. I do this more than I care to confess in an attempt to feel a fraction of what I felt when it happened. And it *did* happen.

"I remember that voice: a delicate yet powerful sound that I felt resonate in my soul. I heard it, Stephanie, *felt* it. I was aware, conscious, and for one single moment in my whole miserable life, I was happy."

"A dream then?"

"The investigator said the car had been opened from the outside. There was no evidence that I had struggled. The airbag had gone off and tests showed it had been cut away with some sort of coral. *Coral,* for fuck sake! Not to mention I woke up on the damn beach with what felt very much like kiss-swollen lips."

"I can't explain it, Eric, but you are a rational man. You must see that this sounds—"

I growl my interruption. "Like I've lost my fucking mind. Yes, I'm well aware of that." Standing, I snatch my jacket from the back of my chair and my keys and wallet from the desk. Striding purposefully toward the door, I'm suddenly tired of this conversation and even more exhausted from wanting that memory to be real, *needing* it like I need my next breath.

"Where are you going?" Stephanie asks as I reach the door, concern etched on her immaculately made up face.

"Home."

"Home?" She asks because my reply really hasn't narrowed it down.

"The castle. I need the solitude." She nods with understanding, and just as the door closes, she rushes to call out.

"You've been drinking Eric. You might not

feel it, and you certainly don't look it, but you are well over the safe limit to drive."

"Maybe, maybe not. And besides, another accident might mean I'll see her again," I mumble to myself, already hoping the weather is a treacherous as it was a month ago.

CHAPTER

Three

M Y KNUCKLES ARE WHITE WITH MY GRIP ON the steering wheel of the replacement Aston Martin Vanquish. The exterior damage to my car was minimal considering it sliced through the metal crash barrier on the bridge and plunged twenty feet into the ocean. The engine, on the other hand, is going to need some serious TLC. I'm thankful the low tide made it possible to retrieve the vehicle at all. Although in all honesty, I hoped the expense of recovering it would have—at the very least—provided some concrete answers to how I got out alive and not burdened me with more questions.

I didn't need to know why the car slid where it did, or how I wasn't able to regain control before I hit the barrier. I didn't care why the barrier failed to do its one job. I don't even want to know how I survived the sheer drop into the ocean, or even how I got out of the sealed car unscathed. I just want to know: *Who* the fuck saved me?

My foot slams on the brake at the far end of the bridge. My castle rises ominously in the distance on the ridge of the cliff face and high above the bridge that connects the mainland to my remote island. A temporary barrier has been erected complete with a multitude of red flashing warning lights. The V12 engine purrs, making the leather seats thrum beneath me. My foot pulses on the gas, igniting a thunderous roar, which mirrors my mood. It's late, dark, and only the absence of a violent storm sets this night apart from that of the accident. My stomach churns, and tight knots pull and scrape painfully at my insides. Blood pumps wildly through my veins, and my heart thumps so loudly I can almost feel it hammering against my rid cage.

I don't do scared. I don't do out of control, and right now, I *don't* trust myself.

Flooring the gas, the car explodes, lurching forward with enough G-force to pin me deep into the seat. The horizon approaches at an alarming speed, and I don't let up. If anything, I press harder on the pedal. The inky backdrop of the night sky bleeds into the pitch-dark ocean below. The myriad of flashing lights ahead melds onto an intense, bright red line. I see the weakened part of the bridge where I crashed through the first time one week ago. The thought makes me jolt. Calm settles in my bloodstream, and I blink slowly, drawing in a steady, final breath. Yes, I mean *final* breath. Decision made. I'm milliseconds away from making the fatal turn of the steering wheel when everything changes.

I. See. Her.

From nowhere, she's in the center of road. In front of me, looking directly at me, and in the fraction of a second it takes for me to pound my foot on the brake, I see everything from that night as clearly as any high definition action movie.

The barrier disintegrating when I hit it. The airbag bursting in my face, knocking me back before the weightless feeling of flying through the air abruptly ends with the car slamming into the ocean. I can feel the water begin to fill the car as it glides so elegantly downward into the darkness. I blink, and when I open my eyes, I see her face on the other side of the window. The headlights are her spotlight, and she looks like a goddess, a silver screen movie star on a watery stage, mesmerizingly beautiful. Her hair moves like inky tendrils, swirling around her body as she darts around the sinking car. Her face is filled with panic, blue eyes large, and her perfect pink lips moving as she calls out something, which is swallowed by the silent ocean. I don't feel her concern, not a bit of it. Why is that? Recalling that moment, I felt completely calm, reconciled maybe. I was going to die, and I was going to die seeing something no one else had ever seen, something magical. A mermaid. I also knew I was dying because I was clearly hallucinating, but it didn't matter. For the first time, I felt at peace, and it was because of *her*.

She saved me. She pulled me from the car and helped me swim to the surface. She lay with me on the beach, her fingers so delicate on my face. And her voice. I'd never heard anything so hypnotic, a melodious sound surely only angels are capable of creating. I felt very much that, in her arms, I was perhaps in heaven. I wished I was. She kissed me; the dream ended, and I was back to my living nightmare, my cursed life.

The tires screech on the tarmac, and I'm grateful for one thing: It isn't raining. The ground isn't wet and slippery because, when I jolt in my seatbelt as the vehicle finally stops, there is no distance at all between the front grill of the car and her trembling bare legs. If the conditions were the same as the night of the accident, I have no doubt we would both be careering off the bridge, me once more in the car, and her plastered over the hood. I shudder with the notion that the former was what I wanted only seconds ago.

I blink several times to make sure the vision before me is real and not something my desperate mind has conjured up. The headlights illuminate her naked body. Her pale skin has this ethereal glow. Her hair is soaked, hanging in damp wavy tendrils almost to her waist. Even in the darkness, her eyes seem to pierce right through me. A turbulent blue saturates her irises, a color the likes of which I've only ever seen in my nightly dreams since the accident.

Blood rushes in my ears so loud I can't hear my own thoughts. *Is it really her?* My hands have this vise-like grip on the steering wheel, and it's an effort to divert my attention away from her enough to gather myself and move.

What if I look away and she disappears?

Get a fucking grip, Eric. She's there, in front of the car, and you're the only one here. Now get out of the fucking car and offer her your damn jacket.

I reach over to the passenger seat and grab my jacket. When I open the car door, she jumps. A nervous, yet happy smile fills her face, and something strange happens inside my chest. An uncomfortable sensation, like some sort of foreign object, is lodged there momentarily. It's not unpleasant, just something new. Ignoring whatever is going on inside me, I step around the front of the vehicle so I am now standing about a foot away from her. She's maybe five foot five, and I'm six feet seven. I don't want to scare the woman. She steps up to me though, closes the distance so there is zero personal space between us and instantly a shit-ton of body heat. I stiffen at the sudden intimacy, and it takes all my effort to remain still when my natural instinct would normally have me holding her at arm's length. If I held her at all, that is.

Still, this feels different, and in the absence of protocol, I decide to go with my gut and just let it happen.

She tips up on her toes to get a closer look. Her hands reach for my cheeks, and she tugs

          THE DIRTY HEROES COLLECTION

me lower so she can look directly into my eyes. Her hands feel like silk on my skin, her touch electrifying dormant parts of my mind and body. She searches my face as if she's looking for something specific. Her brow crinkles in cute little furrowed lines of concentration, and I find I'm holding my breath—with what, I'm not sure. It feels a little like hope. Hope I pass; hope I fit the bill; hope I'm what she is looking for specifically, because I can't ignore the raging inferno coursing through my veins while I wait for the outcome.

Every part of this is new to me. The feeling of uncertainty, the turmoil, the desire to claim, and the feeling of calm. It's chaos in my head right now, yet the only thing I actually *need* is to hear her voice. Then I'll know for sure it's really her.

She's quite breathtaking when she smiles; the purity of it completely illuminates her face, and her eyes shine with wonder and undiluted joy. I feel something slightly more primal toward her, and it's a relief that I seem to have passed whatever test she's just silently conducted.

I slide my jacket over her shoulders, and she shudders under my touch. Her expression is rightly wary; however, she doesn't seem remotely scared. To her, at least, I'm not a dangerous stranger.

"You must be cold." My voice sounds rough, and I have to cough to clear my throat. It doesn't improve the gravelly sound one bit. "Put this on," I add, and when she looks confused, I help her, holding the jacket open so she can see the armholes. She slips her arms through the sleeves. The suit jacket completely drowns her slight frame, and I mentally kick myself when she pulls it across her body, hiding those perky perfect breasts. She shakes her head in what I'm guessing is her response to the first question, even if she's now hugging the jacket to her body. It was an educated assumption, given the external temperature, even if her skin isn't covered in the telltale gooseflesh from the chilly exposure. It's luminescent, flawless, like marble lovingly carved by expert hands.

"What are you doing here? In the middle of nowhere? At night?" Her intense gaze hasn't left mine but she dips her eyes for a fraction of a second. When she looks up slowly through her long dark lashes, she has a shy smile tipping her lips upward. She points her finger in the center of my chest, and I feel more than a spark burst just the other side of her touch. I feel my cock begin to swell and my balls ache. *What the fuck!*

"Me?" I take her finger and watch her pupils dilate. "What's your name?" Her mouth drops, and she sucks in a breath just as I hold mine. *This is it.* She snaps it shut and pats her throat, shaking her head with frustration. "You have a sore throat?" She shakes her head again, patting harder this time.

"You can't speak?" She drops her head; the last negative twist of her head is painfully slow.

My mind races; that can't be true.

Of course it's true.

"Oh." I exhale all the hope I'd held in my lungs.

The surge of emotions, adrenaline, or whatever this is and the aftermath of last week collide, explode, and disintegrate into tiny windswept ashes all around me. It takes a few moments to gather myself as the metaphorical dust settles. I draw in a disjointed breath, my reality snuffing out any remote hope of something changed, of the curse being lifted, of me having a future, having a life. My erection softens, and my pulse returns to normal.

Fairy tales are for little girls and little boys.

I'm not a little boy. This woman is not a little girl, and my reality is the stuff of nightmares, where only twisted souls and demons survive.

This is for the best. I have nothing to offer but a life of pain, and this woman and the woman who saved me deserve better. They both deserve to be worshiped by kings not tortured by a broken prince.

"Do you live near here?" I ask, and she nods.

"Would you like me to take you home? I'll need an address." She vehemently shakes her head and grabs my hands with a sudden rush of panic streaking across her beautiful face. "Okay, okay, so not home." My soothing tone sounds strange and unfamiliar to my ears; nevertheless, it seems to do the trick. She sighs, and the tightness in her face and frame evaporates before me.

My mind is now troubled with the thought of why that might be. Why is going to her home a bad idea? Did someone hurt her? After all, she is naked in the middle of nowhere. Maybe she's run away? My blood pumps violently with a sudden surge of anger, fueled by my imagination and only calmed when I look down at her feet. They look fine, not bloody or bruised from the rough ground or long distances traveled. Another quick appraisal up and down her body and it's clear her skin shows no evidence of trauma. I'm an expert in both inflicting and identifying marks, and I'm happy there are none, or I guess they could've faded by now. How long has she been out here, and why is her hair wet? Did she swim here? My head hurts with the litany of unanswered questions. Exhaustion creeps up my neck and behind my eyes and seeps into every muscle in my body. In an effort to hang on to my sanity, I know I'm going to need answers, and there is only one person who can give those to me. I draw in a deep breath and decide the inquisition can wait until tomorrow.

"You're coming home with me then," I state, my words clipped and in a tone that brooks no argument. Contrary to the response I guess I was expecting, the woman flashes a brilliantly blinding smile and vigorous nod. She steps up flush to me and wraps her surprisingly strong arms around my waist. I was *not* expecting that.

Peeling her arms away from my body I almost laugh when she grins impishly up at me. *Who is this woman?* Pinching my lips together, I fight the urge to smile. The last thing I want to do is encourage her, not when all I want is answers because my mind won't rest, and then to send her on her way. As I walk her round the car to the passenger side, she bites her lip and winces with each step. Maybe the soles of her feet are sore after all? I open the door, and when she climbs in and folds her long slender legs underneath her, I can see that isn't the case.

For a good few seconds, she stares back at me, and it takes another second to register that she's not going to put the seatbelt on. I lean in, place one hand on the seat next to her thigh and, with the other, pull the strap around her body. My face is close to hers, and my gaze locks on those bottomless blues as I blindly search for the holster with the buckle.

She draws in a breath that makes the hairs on my neck spark to life. She exhales slowly. Her sweet breath washes over me, and her eyes darken with obvious pleasure. When I pull back, I notice a steak of blood on her pale thigh. There's a droplet of deep red poised to fall from my watch strap. It must have come loose and the edge is clearly much rougher than I knew. The cut is small but deep and oozes blood. Her chest heaves, and dark desire swirls in the depths of her eyes, and I have never been this hard. She wipes the pooling blood with her finger and sucks it clean. Okay, *now*, I've never been this hard.

She might not be the one who saved me, but she is… No, I have nothing. I have no idea who she is, where she's come from, or what she wants. I've never met anyone like her. I've never experienced a reaction like this to anyone. All I do know is I've never felt this strongly about anything. Whether that is a good thing or not, I'm still undecided, and it wouldn't be a complete lie to say I am more than a little intrigued to find out.

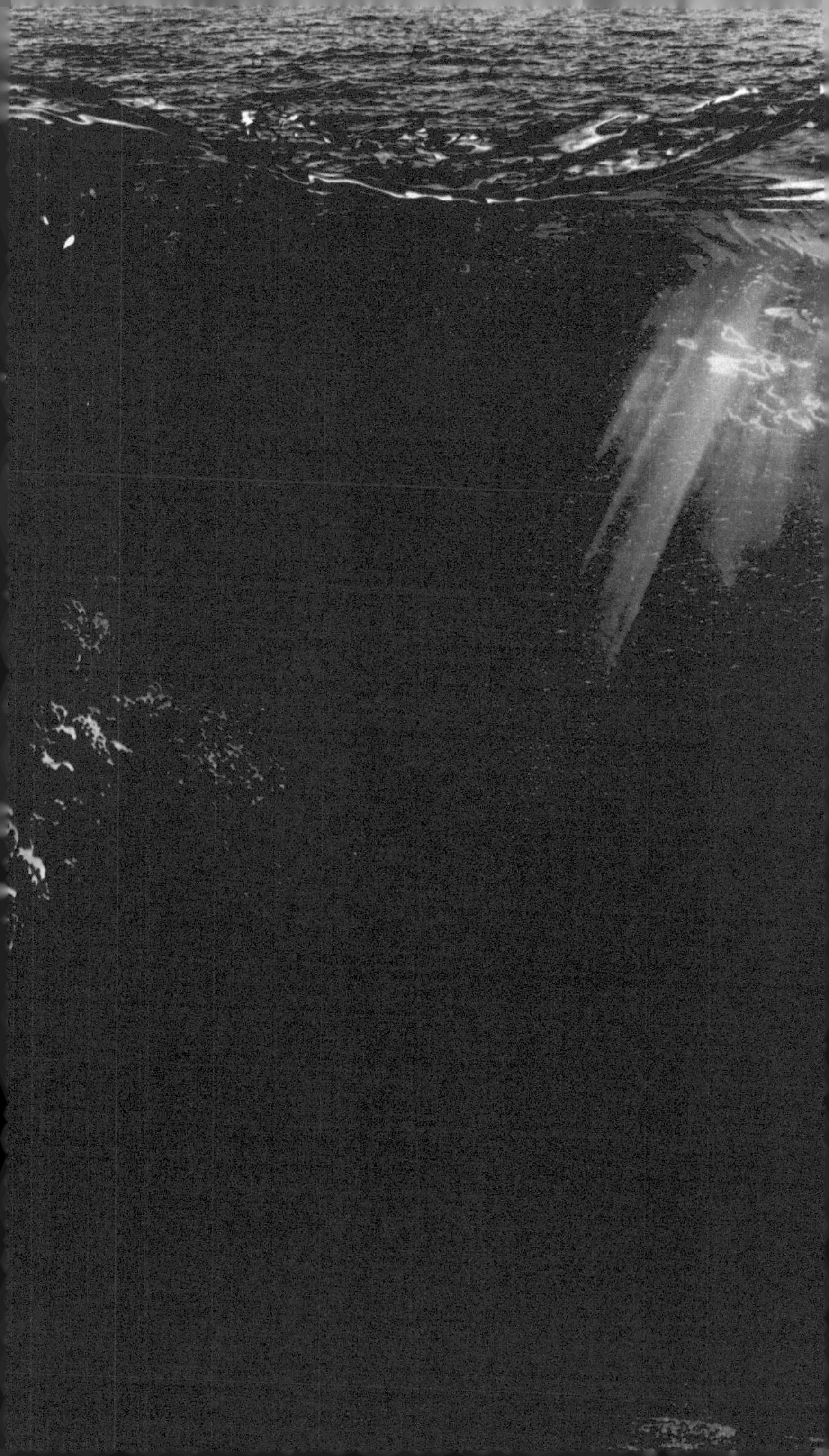

CHAPTER
Four

Two cast iron lanterns, which mark the entrance to the main gate and the start of the land surrounding the castle, are lit. Even from the end of the steep drive, I can see that Winston received my message and has prepared for my unscheduled arrival.

My home is actually the remains of a medieval castle that once stood on this site. The keep is the only habitable part, and although a tenth of the original structure in size, it is still imposing. Impenetrable stone walls tower above us as we approach, blocking out the horizon and transporting me momentarily back to a more primitive time. It's perhaps why I like it here so much. The interior may be more in keeping with the comforts of twenty-first century existence, but outside, it's very much the dark ages. Evidence of real battles marks the building like scars on a warrior. Chips and slashes in the stonework surround the loopholes where archers defended the castle. Soldiers patrolling the crowning battlement on the keep, with it's panoramic view across the land and surrounding the bay, would alert the inhabitants of invaders

Driving under the portcullis, the jaws of the iron gate, unmoved in a hundred years, look very much like teeth set to devour unwelcome visitors. The woman next to me dips and twists her neck to take a better look, her eyes wide with wonder, yet she shivers at the sight. The towering walls enclose a small courtyard, and there are several lights dotted around on each wall where Winston has opened up the rooms as instructed. Winston is the butler I inherited with the property, and despite being a technophobe, he is surprisingly efficient in maintaining this extraordinary property. He doesn't manage all the upkeep himself, but he does manage the subcontracting to ensure it doesn't crumble further into ruin.

The living quarters are spread over several

rooms: study, library, lounge, my own bedroom suite, all comfortably modern. The vast kitchen has a fireplace in which one could roast an entire cow. There is a grand hall, with a minstrels' gallery, and there is a private chapel, all authentic medieval and barely changed in seven hundred years. There are also enough bedchambers to comfortably house twenty guests, if I were so inclined to invite anyone to stay. To date, I have resisted that inclination, *until now.* My eyes dart to the naked thighs, the nervously cupped hands, and the gap in the front of my jacket, exposing her perfect, pert breasts.

What am I doing? This is my place of solitude, my escape, a bolt-hole when I need to get away from life, from work…from people.

Easing off the gas, the car rolls to a stop at the foot of the steep stone steps that lead to the ancient oak front door. Two flaming torches on either side of the door provide some much needed light in the courtyard. I kill the engine and turn to face my guest. Her eyes are like saucers as she peers up at the tower. I guess to many it might look like something from a horror film, but to me it's my sanctuary; it's my home. She catches me staring at her and her cheeks flush with color. I'm reminded of the other color that she sucked clean off her finger, which, in turn, instantly causes my own blood to react, rushing not so much to my cheeks but much farther south.

"I'm not sure this is a good idea," I say out loud and jolt from the strength of her instant grip on my arm and almost hysterical shake of her head. She forces an encouraging smile, her eyes imploring with more depth than words could ever convey. "Okay, okay," I soothe—another first for me—and I get a warm hit in my chest when she visibly relaxes. Pushing down the conflict of emotions currently kicking up a storm inside my head, I blink to break the eye contact and the strange pull she seems to have on me.

"Come on, let's see if Winston has made some of his famous soup. Not sure if you're hungry, but I could definitely eat." My eyes dip to the gap between her legs, where my jacket isn't quite covering her bare pussy. *Yeah, I could definitely eat.*

What the hell is wrong with me? Or maybe I should say: What the hell is *right* with me? I've *never* had these urges. Even in the second best sex dungeon in the city, the most I get is a respite from my constant internal torment. I

	THE DIRTY HEROES COLLECTION

never get sexual satisfaction. I never feel sexual desire. This is unpredicted. I feel like a horny fucking teenage boy, and since I *never* felt like a teenage boy when I *was* a teenage boy, I'm not sure what I should do next.

Closing my eyes, I force myself to ignore the unruly hormones, at least until I can get some answers. My jaw clenches with the effort, and my skin prickles with the itch to touch her. I reach for the door instead and leap from the car as if my seat has been suddenly lit by the fiery flames of hell. Walking round the car, I use the precious seconds and drop in temperature to cool my burning desire and regain some control. I open her door, offering my hand to assist and manage to keep my wandering gaze away from falling between her legs. She stands and instantly buckles with silent pain, agony contorting her face as she clings to my arms to support her weight. I don't know what's happened. She didn't look to be in pain when I first saw her. When she stood in the road, I wasn't aware of any injury. I guess the adrenaline of facing down a speeding car might have masked the pain, and now that the danger is over, whatever is causing this reaction is back in full force.

I secure my arm around her waist and take most of her weight, helping her to stand. Her eyes darken, and if I'm not mistaken, something other than pain masks a hidden smile. *No, that can't be right; I'm mistaken.* I lift her into my arms and relish the way her body folds against mine. A happy silent sigh escapes from her soft pink lips, curved upward with a sweet smile, and I'm once again transported to another time, a love-struck teenager this time, and I'm not sure which manifestation is more disturbing to me.

The front door creaks open and a warm slash of light strikes us, illuminating the way inside. Winston's face is a picture, impassive yet curious.

"Would you like me to take your jacket, sir?" he says after closing the door behind us, his tone disinterested. He barely glances at the woman in my arms. I arch my brow high, fighting the urge to laugh when I realize he was joking.

This is so strange that, for a moment, I have to consider whether I did actually die in that accident or I have somehow slipped into another dimension, because this is some seriously weird shit going on.

"Thank you, Winston, but that won't be necessary."

"Very good, sir. Would you like some supper? I have some crème de legumes soup prepared, or I could make you a sandwich."

"Soup would be great, thanks."

"And for your guest?" he asks, warmly addressing the woman in my arms.

"She'll have the same. She doesn't speak." My comment is absorbed by those knowing grey eyes, but he treats it as I would expect, that it doesn't concern him.

"I'll bring it right away. I lit the fire in the study…unless you would prefer the dining room?"

"The study is fine. And if you could make up the guest room when you're done, that would be great."

"Very good, sir. I have to say it's very nice to see."

"What? That I have a guest, or that I'm carrying her in my arms?"

"Neither. Actually, sir, I was going to say it's very nice to see you smile." His lips crack a wry smile. He holds my narrowed stare as if he is expecting a backlash at his impudence and is equally happy to take it on the chin.

"That will be all, Winston." I'm tempted but decide an impassive dismissal is best. It's bad enough dealing with this creature in my arms let alone insubordination in the ranks, even if it is well meaning.

The vibrations of her light laugh ripple through me like a warm current, and I have to physically shake myself from the unsettling reactions she seems to evoke in me—at least until I can figure out who the hell she is and what she wants.

I stride across the flagstones of the cavernous entrance hall, through the arched hall toward my study. Using my elbow on the lever arch door handle, I back into the room in lieu of kicking the door open since my arms are occupied. Winston has set an impressive fire blazing, and I walk over and place her carefully in one of the winged back chairs that face the fire. When I relinquish my hold, she whimpers, not the actual sound, everything but the sound. The way her jaw drops, slack with the sudden exhale, her lips trembling as her body visibly shudders at my absence. She grasps for my hand and entwines her fingers with mine with something akin to feral desperation, her eyes pleading with me to remain close.

I'm at a loss. I don't ever appease people the way I feel I need to with her. No, not just

   THE DIRTY HEROES COLLECTION

appease; I *want* to comfort her, protect her, and yes, I want to hurt her too.

And there it is. My ugly demon in all its glory. My insides churn with the burning need to do my worst. Torment and agony fill every cell in my body until I'm consumed with it, driven by it, my own personal hell. She's the picture of innocence. Unblemished, pure and vulnerable, and I want to mark her, dominate her. I want to *hurt* her.

I turn away, snatching my hand from hers. She has no idea who she's dealing with, and since she's the one that is actually lost, I need to be the one to put her straight, maintain some boundaries, for her own good. The last thing this fragile human needs is a monster like me.

I draw in a fortifying breath. It's ridiculous to me that I need to be drawing on some mystical inner strength to simply walk away, but I do. I take a few strides to the door, and when I hear her light steps behind me, I spin around. She's walking slowly toward me, my jacket a crumpled pile of material in the seat behind her. Her slender body trembles as she takes each tentative step toward me, her eyes fixed on mine, and I find I'm utterly mesmerized. Her skin looks smooth as porcelain, delicate and flawless. The curve of her hips, narrow waist and firm swell of her breasts make my mouth water, my cock stir, and my palm twitch. Then I notice something I've only ever seen when I am playing—a slice of unadulterated pain dances in the crystal blue eyes she fixes on me.

"It hurts to walk?" I ask. She nods once, raises her chin and takes another defiant step, embracing the pain that is clearly shooting from her feet through her body. Her pupils dilate to large dark orbs filled with desire, and by the time she is flush to me, she's the picture of wanton. My ragged breaths drown out the loud pounding in my chest. She tilts her head as if she's waiting for me to ask another question. I have only one, yet I can't bring myself to ask it. Not when I want to hear the answer so badly.

No, no I won't go there. It's adrenaline and trauma, nothing more. She doesn't want this; no one wants this.

I bend and thrust my shoulder into her soft midsection. Lifting her high, the tension in her body resembles that of a surfboard, stiff, a little unbalanced, and completely out of place in my study. I drop her back into the chair and scowl.

"Don't fucking move then." My low grumble sounds more petulant than angry. Still, she visibly balks at the tone, and I feel like a shit for losing my temper. She's clearly been through a lot, and despite what my mind is racing with, she's not *my* victim to torture. She needs to eat, get some rest, clothes, and then she needs to leave me the hell alone.

When I turn this time, I don't hesitate at the door. I walk out and pull it closed behind me. This is all wrong. What I'm feeling, what I want from her, what I think I've seen in her eyes, it's all lies. I've lived long enough with this curse to know there is no happy ending for me. Pain and suffering are my only gifts, and even *I* am not that much of a monster to inflict that on her.

I pass Winston in the hall, carrying a tray of soup, some bread that looks to be fresh out of the oven, and an open bottle of my Grand Cru, Cote de Nuits. At five thousand a bottle I'm not surprised he's raising his grey bushy brow when I block his path.

"Are we celebrating, Winston? Because if that's the case, I have a bottle of ship wrecked champagne in the cellar that Christie's valued at seven million."

"I thought about it, sir, but decided that would be better suited to your wedding day." His flat response is poorly timed.

"Tell me, Winston… Do you enjoy working here?" I snap.

"Very much, sir. Would you like me to get the champagne?" Impassive and polite. I feel my fists curl at his amused aloofness.

"Are you trying to piss me off?"

"Just trying to anticipate your every whim, sir, as always."

"Well, my whim is for you *not* to try my patience." I grab a bread roll from the tray and walk past my bemused and somewhat smug looking butler.

"Will you be joining the young lady shortly?" he calls out.

"No, I'm going to my quarters."

"What about the young lady?" I can hear the disappointment in his voice, and at that moment, I make my decision. I don't alter my gait when I reply.

"If she's not hungry, find her some clothes, give her some money, and kick her out."

"What about the guest room?"

"Out!" I yell as I reach the end of the long corridor.

"You don't mean that, sir." His voice echoes off the walls and rolls around with the uncomfortable feeling in my gut.

"Do I look like I'm joking? Your choice, Winston. You either show her the door, or you can both leave together."

"Very good, sir." He nods and smoothly turns his back before I can see the certain condemnation in his eyes. *Fuck him. It's the right decision.*

CHAPTER
Five

I TAKE THE SPIRAL STAIRCASE TWO AT A TIME AND thunder down the corridor, frustration, confusion, and raw rage bubbling through my bloodstream like lava. My footsteps echo like a stone army on my heels, only falling silent when I enter the master bedroom suite. A large square room, stone walls a meter thick disappearing into the heavans above me. Even with the mezzanine slicing the wall fifteen feet above my head for part of the room, the ceiling is incredibly high. Winston has set a small fire in here and has my favorite whiskey and crystal glass tumbler laid out next to my armchair. This room is my sanctuary, untouched and unchanged in a hundred years. A scattering of several different sofas, occasional tables and several oriental rugs soften the feel of the room. On two of the walls hang large intricate tapestries depicting local battles, dating back to the eighteenth century.

The mezzanine, however, is a different story. I empty my pockets on the writing desk near the door and walk over to grab the un-opened whiskey bottle before heading up the open oak staircase that edges the room. My canopy bed dominates the far wall. The wall opposite is banked with seven video monitors above my hi-tech desk.

Kicking my shoes off and loosening my belt buckle, I grab the TV remote and sit on the end of the bed, torn between craving the alcohol and needing to see what's going on downstairs. My curiosity wins. I fire up the monitors and quickly scan the array of images that fill all the screens. All rooms, corridors, alcoves, internal and external, every possible angle of the castle is covered and recorded. I select the study, which instantly illuminates the largest of the screens, a sixty-inch image with surround sound fills my senses. There she is. Why do I feel relief, when I've told Winston she has to leave? Why the hell am I happy she's sitting with Winston? In my

　　THE DIRTY HEROES COLLECTION

jacket, eating my food, being comforted by my butler.

"Would you like some wine?" Winston holds the bottle up and motions to the empty glass on the tray he placed on the table just in front of her. She looks at him, a shy smile and tentative nod has him filling her glass with red wine, *expensive* red wine. She takes the glass and gulps the liquid completely down, gasping for air and holding it out for a refill before Winston has had the chance to replace the bottle on the tray.

"Oh my, you were thirsty. Maybe you should drink some water too." Winston pours some more wine, not quite so much this time and then offers her a glass of water. She drinks the wine and sips the water, alternating and staring at Winston as if seeking some sort of approval.

"So, you don't speak but you understand English?"

She nods, and I find myself leaning forward, intrigued and irritated that I didn't think to ask her this question, or any questions for that matter. I was too consumed with my selfish primal desires to take a moment and learn something about her. *Too fucking scared by my own reactions.* I have to remind myself none of it really matters. However curious I am, I still did the right thing.

"Do you know sign language?" Winston places the wine bottle down and uses his hands to—I assume—ask the same question with sign language. Her brows furrow and she shakes her head.

"Right, yes, and no questions it is then." He claps his hands together and settles back into the chair opposite her. She picks at the bread, dunking in it messily into the soup and leaning close to the bowl so she can scoop the liquid into her mouth. Winston hands her a spoon, which she holds in the other hand but doesn't use.

"Do you live close by?" She nods.

"Do you have family?" She nods.

"Have you run away from home?" She hesitates. Her mouth pinches to one side as she considers her answer. A moment later, she nods her head but it was clearly more complicated than a straight answer.

"Why have you come here?" Nice one, Winston, you idiot. That's hardly a yes or no question. She points to the door and then my jacket.

"You came for Eric? Do you know him?"

    THE DIRTY HEROES COLLECTION

Winston's tone is pitched with surprise. I don't blame him. She nods again, and my jaw nearly hits the floor.

"How? How do you know him?" Winston sounds genuinely confused, and it's only a fraction of what I feel.

Yes, answer him, how do you know me? It can't have been you that saved me, can it? Maybe the voice I heard that night was all in my head.

I find I'm holding my breath, waiting for her to mime the events of the accident, some elaborate and dramatic reenactment, which would confirm I am not going mad, that I did see what I saw, and that she is the *one*.

She shrugs and continues to guzzle down the food. I'm deflated and a little pissed.

"Well, I'm afraid Master Eric doesn't want to play." Winston's sarcastic comment and derisive tone is lost on her. She blinks several times, long lashes sweeping her pale cheekbones, and she tilts her head to one side. Winston sighs. He clarifies, "You can't stay here." She drops the lump of bread in the soup, and her hands fly to her panic stricken face. This time it's not only her head shaking, her whole body trembles. She stares at Winston, and I can see from his straightened shoulders and his troubled brow that he's extremely uncomfortable at her obvious distress. "I'm sorry, Miss. I will get you some fresh clothes, but then you'll have to leave," he explains. She holds up three fingers, I'm not sure what she's trying to say.

"Three what, my dear? You need to say three things?" he asks and she shakes her head. "You need to get three things from him?" Again no. "You need to stay three days?" She claps her hands, her smile brighter than a burst of sunshine breaking over the horizon. "You need to stay here for three days and then what? You'll leave?" Her smile vanishes and her eyes glaze. She sucks in a long breath and straightens herself in the chair. Turmoil flits across her face. She blinks, bites her lip, and forces a pained and tragic smile when she nods.

"I can ask again for you, but I know Eric, and I would not hold your breath," Winston offers, resigned at her misplaced optimism. She takes his hand and presses the back of it to her cheek, swaying slightly with girlish glee. He picks up the tray, and she grabs the bottle of wine and glass before he is out of reach, grinning like the cat that got the cream. "I'll ask," Winston mutters and walks from the room cloaked with a solemn air of inevitability. I never change my mind. *Ever.*

I don't bother to follow Winston as he leaves the study. I use the zoom on the camera located high in the corner of the room to close in on my guest. With shaky hands, she pours another glass of wine and stands, looking around the room as if seeing it for the first time. Her impossibly large eyes, full of wonder and curiosity, seem to sparkle as pain slices across her soft facial features when she walks. Just as before, after the initial bite, she seems to embrace the sensation like an old and welcome friend. Sliding her bare feet on the smooth flagstones, she glides across the room. Letting my jacket fall from her shoulders, her white gold hair, now dry, sways with every sensual step, and I can't help getting the feeling she knows I'm watching. She owns the room. The vast space diminishes to nothing, and all I can see is her.

She touches everything with keen interest, every object, every picture, even the rug, which she drops to her knees to inspect more closely. Wine spills from the glass, and when she dips her nose to the floor and licks the puddle of red liquid clean off the floor. I'm both grossed out and turned on with the sublime act of submission. *If only I had told her to do that.* Fuck.

My cock swells, and I shuffle back to rest my back on the head board, unzip my fly, and ease my straining erection free and into my waiting hand. She places the glass on the floor and jumps to her feet. Her mouth drops open with a silent cry. Biting her lip, she closes her eyes. Her nipples tighten with the rush of obvious pleasure. She squeezes her breasts, and I do the same to my cock. I moan with the sweet agony of this new sensation assaulting my senses.

Sexual desire surges through my veins, ignited by the sight unfolding before me. My grip tightens, and I firmly stroke my length, absorbed by this woman in my study. Her effect on me is intoxicating. I can't look away, and I can only pray that Winston gets sidetracked, because I need this.

She wanders over to the antique maple pedestal desk with ox blood leather inlay, seemingly mesmerized by the single flame dancing in the ornate silver candlestick holder. She perches her bottom on the edge of the desk. Pulling her legs up, she slides over to the center, picking up the candlestick and stretching her legs out in front of her in one seamless and extremely sensual movement that has my balls aching for release already. She wiggles her toes

   THE DIRTY HEROES COLLECTION

playfully before lying fully back, stretching herself taut with a slight arc to her spine. *Fuck!*

This is not the first time I've watched a beautiful woman from afar. It's not the first time I've had a naked woman spread out like this. It isn't even the first time I've watched without their knowledge. This is the first time, however, I'm hard as fucking nails because of it. Blood surges, swelling the tip of my cock to a painful deep purple color, and I have to admit I don't think I've ever been this turned on. My mouth goes dry watching her lift the candle high and tip the flame toward her navel. The wax drips easily, flowing like milk from the ivory candle. Her back arches when the first drop hits her skin.

My own cock weeps with arousal at the beautiful sight. I sweep my thumb over the crown and slick the pre-cum over and down my shaft making my strokes a little easier. She splatters a pattern over her abdomen, down to her public bone and back up to her heaving breasts. She must be in agony. That isn't a safety candle, and as far as I know, she doesn't have a protective layer of oil coating her skin. She writhes, and her eyes glaze, her breath shallow and panting. One hand reaches between her legs, and I curse that I didn't see fit to install cameras from the other end of the study. Still, it's pretty obvious that she has sunk at least one finger inside herself. Her greedy hips begin to rotate and she grinds against the heel of her hand like she's possessed. My own hand is ferociously jerking my cock, a mix of anger and raw animal desire coursing through me. I pump my fist in time with her eager hips. Her body is covered in white streaks of drying wax. The image is stunning, marred only by the wish that it was my come making those marks.

I have the volume on full, desperate to hear her cries, hear her scream in obvious ecstasy. Frantic breaths and hips bucking hard on to the desktop are the only audible sounds, that and my own moans and grunts of erotic frustration. I want to make her moan, I want to make her writhe. Fuck it. I want to make her scream my fucking name.

My balls tighten, and the fire at the very base of my spine seizes me all of a sudden, intense and uncontrollable. At that critical moment, I look at the screen. Her head is thrown back, her eyes wide open, and she's staring directly at the camera, as if staring right at me, I explode. My climax streams across the bed in thick white

    THE DIRTY HEROES COLLECTION

ribbons. I can't look away from the screen, she's taut, her body arched and frozen. Her hand is locked between her thighs as she squeezes the last of her own release from her body. The candle is broken in two in her hand, the flame extinguished at some point in the throes of her orgasm.

Tension leaves her body in a loud slump of bones and flesh hitting the desk, and she lets out a heavy breath. She rolls onto her stomach and unashamedly peers up through long lashes and white golden hair that has fallen over her face. Her cheeks are flushed the perfect dusky pink, and her lips look so swollen they really need to be kissed. I shake myself, disgusted with the thought.

What the fuck, Eric? You don't kiss.

There's a knock on the door below, and it takes a moment to remember Winston was on his way to ask me something he already knows the answer to. I wipe my hand on my trousers. Get up from the bed and strip. My head is a mess. What the hell just happened? Honestly, I can't figure it out. Who the fuck is she? What has she done to me? I'm drifting on an ocean of the unknown. Drawn to this siren like a sailor to the rocks. I know I should send her away. But part of me wants to test her, wants to see if she's real. She said she came for me. Well, I guess its time for her to prove it.

I jog down the stairs and grab my robe from the back of the door before I open it. Winston is holding one of my t-shirts and a pair of my jogging bottoms, neatly folded, with one of my waterproof jackets over the crook of his arm.

"Is it all right to give the lady these clothes of yours? There really isn't anything in the castle suitable," he asks flatly.

"Yes, that's fine, and give her some money too. Five hundred. You think that's enough?" I pick my wallet from the top of the writing desk, take a fistful of notes and hand them to Winston.

"I think she just wants to stay, sir. I don't believe she wants your money." Distaste curls his lips, and my temper bristles with the inference.

"I didn't say she wants my money. I asked if you thought five hundred is enough to help her out."

"Yes, sir. I am sure that will be plenty." He takes the money between his thumb and finger as if it's somehow infected. "Will there be anything else?"

"No." My jaw grinds with tension.

"Very good, sir." He hesitates and I can see the weight of the next words is heavy on him. Still, not heavy enough that he keeps his opinion to himself. "Are sure you want to do this?"

"It's not a question of *want*, Winston. I *need* to do this." He raises his sardonic brow but nods curtly before he turns away and walks back down the corridor.

"Well, good night then. Sleep well," he mutters.

"I heard that tone, Winston." There are so few people in my life for this very reason. They couldn't possibly understand.

"Good," he says, and I slam the door.

Fuck him. What does he know anyway?

CHAPTER
Six

Dropping my head on the door, the painful thud does nothing to knock some sense into me. What am I doing? I've had my first ever hard-on induced by an actual person, and I'm sending her away. Couldn't I just be normal for one fucking minute and—oh, I don't know—just fuck her, like any other red blooded Neanderthal.

Because you're not normal, and you need her pain, her true pain, and you know, despite what you've seen so far, that that doesn't exist. Stop fooling yourself and just go back to porn.

I bang my head one more time to punctuate my conclusion.

I make my way back up to my bedroom,

I am more than familiar dealing with; the latter is new, and frankly, I'm getting pretty fucking sick of these new feelings. By the time I reach the top of the stairs, I can see Winston is back in the study with his back turned to my guest. She's still naked, her body streaked with red burn marks and traces of wax, which crumble and fall to the floor with every shaky breath she's taking. She stares at the pile of clothes on the floor, her eyes filled with unshed tears.

"I'm sorry, Miss, but you have to leave. Put these clothes on. I'd call a taxi for you, but no one will come out this time of night. I'm afraid I don't drive, and well, Eric… I'm sorry." He jolts when her hand slips into his. She's nigh on downed by the excess material of my clothes, looking so small, fragile, and lost, I feel the first prick of a blade of regret puncture my chest.

"I have to do this." The words rattle, hollow and trite.

She tugs his arm and leads *him* to the door. An understanding smile barely makes her lips curl; nevertheless, it's there, and Winston seems to appreciate it.

"Here. He wanted you to have this." Winston passes her the notes. She takes them, screws

THE DIRTY HEROES COLLECTION

them in her hand, and as she walks through the door Winston holds open, she drops them in the bin. A silly test. Still, I release the breath I was holding all the same. I follow them down the corridor. Winston can't seem to help himself being the congenial guide, explaining how old the castle is, dropping names of prominent battles fought, and highlighting some of the rare pieces salvaged and preserved for posterity. The woman smiles and nods, right up to the point he opens the front door and she steps outside.

"I am very sorry, Miss." He bends down to take his house shoes off and hands them to her. "I'm afraid there really isn't anything suitable for your dainty feet, but these will offer some protection against the cobblestones." She takes the shoes and, to his surprise, leans up and kisses his cheek. He mutters something I can't hear. I scroll the clip back and slow the film, catching the shape of his lips and words more clearly. I don't think I've ever heard him say a cross word, and now I'm a motherfucker all of a sudden. Maybe not so sudden, and in fairness, looking at this sorry sight descending the front steps, I have to agree with his accurate assessment. Besides, I've been called worse.

The spotlight cutting a slither in the darkness

and splashing light across the courtyard vanishes when Winston closes the door. It takes a moment to adjust my eyes to the dark. Slowly the image becomes more visible, as the lit rooms dotted around the castle illuminate the courtyard. The woman passes my car, carrying Winston's shoes in one hand, walking barefoot across the flint cobblestones, smiling with every painful step until she reaches the center of the square. There is a brilliant flash of light and a crack of thunder so loud it shakes the glass in the windows. A sudden torrent of rain falls from the sky, instantly drenching the woman. Each drop falling so hard it kicks high off the ground with the rebound.

She starts to peel out of her clothes. She dropped the coat to the ground as soon as she stood still. The t-shirt is dark and heavy with water, clinging to her curves, and it sticks to her as she lifts it over her face. The sweatpants are sliding off her hips as it is; a little extra weight from the rain means she only has to shake a little and they pool on the ground. She steps free of them, and instead of standing on the material to protect her feet from what must be sharp flint and the chill of the ground, she kicks them away from her. Dropping her head back, she looks up

  THE DIRTY HEROES COLLECTION

to the sky, welcoming the icy rain with open arms.

What the hell?

I drop the remote control and walk over to the window. The ledge is wide enough to sit comfortably, and I do just that, sit and stare at the incredible sight below. Beauty and pain in all its stunning glory. I'm speechless and unbelievably turned on. She shivers, and even from here, I can see the telltale prickles of gooseflesh. Her nipples look impossibly hard, and her skin glows, slick with the wintry rain. She's must be freezing, even numb with the inevitable cold. She's going to be suffering every second of such exposure to these extreme elements. Not to mention the constant pain tearing through her from her feet upward. How long can she endure this before she catches pneumonia? How long am I going to let her suffer? *Forever*. This is her choice, not mine, and the pleasure etched on her face would indicate she's in no hurry to change her mind.

Her eyes are closed, facing the downpour for endless minutes. I'm transfixed. She shudders, sweeps her head forward and then arches back. Her long hair, soaked, sprays droplets of water in a shower around her. She slicks it back, smoothing it out of her face with both hands. Her eyes are still closed. She opens her mouth and sticks her tongue out, catching raindrops like they were nectar. She licks her lips and drops her chin. Drawing in a deep breath, I find I mirror her breathing until I feel the tension of it in my lungs. Then, she looks up, and I feel like I've been hit with a cannon. I gasp for another breath. Her eyes bore into me as if there is no distance. I see her, and I fucking know she sees me. I feel the connection on an elemental level, an understanding, a truth.

She's doing this for me.

Part of me is relieved; part is fucking terrified, and part of me wants to run downstairs and end her suffering, but that's not how this works. I want her suffering, and she wants to give it to me. I open the window.

"Dance for me." I call down. My order causes her to swallow slowly. She glances around at the uneven ground and then back at me. My cock is already twitching, and when she sucks in her bottom lip, desire making her breath come faster in little pants, I am rock-fucking-hard in my hand.

She pitches up on her toes and leaps forward, sweeping her arms around her body like a flame.

Her breasts bounce with every undulation as she curves and contorts her body every which way. She dances across the courtyard, spinning, twirling, arching and flying gracefully to the sound of the thunderstorm raging above her. Her movements are enthralling, captivating and spellbinding all at once. When she folds to the floor with her final movement, I'm breathless. The blood pouring from her feet is washed away by the torrential rainfall. She gasps for air, her chest heaving and her body wracked with exhaustion.

"Again." I demand flatly. Without hesitation, she rises like a phantom. Her arms stretch above her as if in prayer, her lithe body an apparition of perfection. Her muscles taut and trembling with exertion, she once more performs what has to be a routine devised by angels to please the gods. She dances and dances, again and again and again. Each time she collapses, I resist the urge to go to her. Each time harder than the last. The hours pass and realization dawns on me, just as the day is about to break. The faint warm glow on the horizon threatens to shatter the darkness cloaking us both. As much as she has suffered, I have been with her, watching, keeping my focus only on her. This was a test.

She didn't break; she blossomed. And I finally understand. She won't ever stop. Not until I tell her to.

Retreating from the window as she continues to spin, leap and prance around the courtyard, I slip my jeans on, and snatching the fur throw from the end on my bed, I head downstairs. The front door creaks, groaning my presence loud enough to make her falter. Weakness causes her to stumble to her knees. Closing the distance in long determined strides, I drop to one knee and tip her lowered chin. Her eyes sparkle with pleasure. Her lips tremble, and I almost do it. She wants me to, wants my kiss like her life depends on it, but I can't. I won't. I don't *ever* kiss. She looks so fucking tragic, powerfully so. I have to force my eyes shut as the desire to crash my lips to hers surges like a tidal wave inside me. I can almost taste her sweetness as my tongue dives in, demanding everything, her compliance, her desire, her pain. I want it, all of it. Blood rushes in my ears. Heat tears through me like a wildfire, and my cock strains in the confines of my tight jeans. Something's got to give, and after her amazing display of obedience, I may have to concede, this time, it might have to be me.

"You want me?" I ask. She blinks, and for a moment, I have to wonder, who the hell would? The hit in my chest when she nods feels like an atom bomb exploding. Her shy smile fair does me in. "Okay, but I have to warn you, this…this is just the beginning." She tips her chin high, defiant and proud. I snatch it, pull it low and pinch the skin between my thumb and forefinger. Her eyes glaze and widen with raw desire. "Just the beginning." Repeating the words on an exhale, I watch her shiver from head to toe. She sucks her bottom lip into her mouth, through her teeth. Biting down when she pulls back, she licks her lips and touches the fresh blood with her fingertips. Holding her finger up, the dark red looks almost black in the dawn light. She watches, fascinated as the drop starts to roll slowly down her finger. Before it reaches her knuckle, she has it pressed to her mouth, and flicking her tongue, she swipes any traces clean, her pupils as dark as the thoughts race through my mind.

"So it begins."

CHAPTER
Seven

SHE WEIGHS NEXT TO NOTHING IN MY ARMS as I carry her back inside. Her skin is drenched with a tempting mixture of rain and sweat. Tears streak her flushed face, and I find myself distracted with the desire to drink them down. Such beauty, such sacrifice. I don't think I've ever witnessed anything quite so humbling. I never believed it possible—part of me still doesn't, even if I did witness it with my own eyes. She silenced my demons and awakened something so raw and primal, I felt it vibrate through me, rattling my mind and shaking my very foundations. Everything I know, everything I hold true is in turmoil because of this woman.

Primal passion courses in my veins like liquid fire. Feral lust threatens to shatter the tentative control I have on this unpredicted situation, and honestly, I don't know what I want to do first: devour or worship, fuck or feast.

I kick the door to my bedroom suite wide open. She tenses in my arms, desire so strong it must feel a good deal like anger rolling off me in waves. She looks up, eyes wide with worry, and I get a jolt, a hard hit in my chest. She should fear me; still, this type of worry is strangely uncomfortable. Normally, I don't care. This is different again, and I'm struggling to know what exactly has changed.

There are some things I won't compromise on, and others, for the first time, I am feeling more inclined to at least consider. I won't kiss her, but I do care enough to soothe, to comfort. The sexual attraction is new and volatile, like a powder keg of carnality, a Pandora's box just opened and I can't wait to explore. However, I crave her pain for other reasons, and I need to know if her pleasure from it is *real*.

I carry her into the bathroom and sit her on the vanity unit next to the double copper sink.

"Don't move and don't touch anything."

    THE DIRTY HEROES COLLECTION

My voice is hoarse, rough enough without the abrasive tone. "I'm going to run a bath and clean up your feet," I add more softly. She swallows slowly, and her lips curve in a breathtakingly sweet smile. I turn away and start the water in the oversized tub, pour some bath oil, and then start searching in the cupboard for some first aid supplies. Honestly, I've never even looked in these cupboards. I just assume Winston is the sort of butler that would keep the appropriate supplies in the appropriate places, and lo, there it is, one fully equipped first aid box.

I move her, so her back is flush to the mirror so she can stretch her legs out in front and I can get a better look at her feet. It's difficult to see the extent of the damage. Dried blood is mixed with grit and dirt and ground into her flesh. My first assessment is that it's considerable. I run a mix of lukewarm water and antiseptic in the sink and lower her feet in. She doesn't flinch. Her eyes roll to the heavens, and she exhales a breathy sound that goes right to the base of my cock.

"That doesn't hurt?" I ask. She nods. "You like pain?" She boldly takes my hand and places it between her legs. My fingers instantly curl and seek somewhere warm and wet to hide. I'm not disappointed. "Yes, I would say you enjoy pain." My voice drops an octave with nefarious intent. It's an effort to concentrate on the task in hand. The water is as dark as if it were filled with only her blood, and I can't describe the sick sensations of pleasure creeping into the darkest crevices of my mind.

"Who are you? What's your name?" She shakes her head, suddenly looking irritated or perhaps disappointed, as if I've asked the wrong question. "Why are you here?" She smiles this time and places her free hand in the center of my chest. Her palm may as well have been a pure bolt of lightning from the shock to my body. "Me? Why me?" She tilts her head coquettishly; her pupils dilate, and she shamelessly grinds against the fingers I have inside her. *Fuck!*

In that moment I don't care why, who, or what happens next. In this moment, I feel like a weight is lifting. I am able to shuck the cloak of despair that has been my burden to carry for as long as I can remember. I decide to embrace these new feelings, every fucking one of them.

I sink my fingers deeper. Using my free hand, I fist her hair and yank her head back. Her neck is exposed, and I lick the taut elegant line of tendon from her collarbone to just under the ear. Her whole body shivers, and on the return journey, I bite down. She convulses as I suck with all my might. I feel the draw in my toes, pulling her skin into my mouth and gorging on the silky softness. I can't get enough. She bucks on my fingers, her own sound of wetness masked slightly by the sloshing of her feet in the sink. She grips my shoulders, anchoring me to her. Her panting breaths are rapid, like hunted prey finally caught. I pull back enough to watch her face as she begins to come apart in my hands. Her mouth gapes with wanton abandon, and I don't think I've seen anything so mesmerizing. Her inner muscles clamp around my fingers, tight and pulsing as she climbs higher, dizzy and delirious, falling only when I ease the pressure of my dexterous fingers.

Her eyelids flutter, and she takes a few dissociated glances around the room before settling back on me. I don't think I've ever seen that color blue in a pair of eyes before. They seem to change in the light, a hypnotic spectrum of deepest blue to light aquamarine with facets of white light that seem to pierce right through me. I ease my fingers out and chuckle when she silently whimpers at the loss. Holding my fingers up, I arch my brow, glance at the glossy sheen of her arousal and back to her. She licks her lips and opens her mouth. She sucks them clean, drawing them into her hot mouth the instant I place them on her flat tongue. My cock stirs, swelling painfully behind the loose constraints of my sweat pants. Her gaze drops, and as much as I want to sink into her right now, I've decided I need to be sure. The test isn't quite over. This is more than a fuck. This is more than a play session. This is so much more. I feel it at a cellular, spiritual level.

"Right. Let's look at you feet." I say, matter-of-factly. She pulls her knees to her chest, elevating her feet free of the sink. Blood trickles into the bowl; however, the slashes and lacerations don't look so bad. In fact, they hardly look like cuts at all, a few deeper red marks but the open wounds that were there just a moment ago have vanished.

"Wow, you heal fast." I pat the soles of her feet dry with a soft towel. There's barely any blood at all. She pulls her feet away from my scrutinizing stare and shrugs lightly. She reaches for the waistband of my joggers. I capture her slender but surprisingly strong fingers in one hand.

"Nah-ah. Patience. Don't think for one

moment you are going to get what you want just because you are here in my bathroom. We are still doing this, whatever this is, *my way*. Understand?" She sits back and bows her head with contrition, only she doesn't quite hold the submissive pose without peeking up through long lashes at the last second, a mischievous grin pulling her lips upward like she's gotten exactly what she wants.

We'll see. It's going to be a long day and night.

I scoop her off the counter and plop her into the deep bath. I'm about to turn the taps off, but she dives her head under the flow. Silently laughing, the water fills her mouth. She coughs and splutters, and when she's caught her breath, she does it again until I turn them off.

She's crazy, spellbinding. Utter joy lights her face brighter than a supernova. Rolling, and writhing in the large tub, she's a picture of childish innocence, perfectly mixed with delicious deviance. She kneels up, and the bubbles swirl and soak her skin, as oil-infused water clings to her body like a sensual slick of pure temptation. She slides back onto her bottom, swishing her arms this way and that, creating wave after wave of bubbles, filling the room with fragrant jasmine and pomegranate. I'm tempted to sit and watch her simply enjoy herself playing in the tub; however, she pantomimed something about three days to Winston, so the time for games has passed.

I walk to the door. A loud splash halts my exit. She's on her feet, bubbles distractedly racing down her curves. Her skin is pink from the heat of the water, and my palm twitches with envy. Her brows are pulled together with concern, and I have to wave her down when she tries to get out of the tub.

"Whoa there. Stay, stay and enjoy the bubbles. I won't be long."

She tilts her head but doesn't lower herself into the water. I walk back and push down on her shoulders. She sinks to her knees and tips her chin up. Her eyes are wide with wonder, searching my face as if seeing it for the first time. I can't express what havoc that level of intensity is wreaking on my sanity. I take her chin in my thumb and forefinger, and my gaze falls to her lips, soft, wet and so fucking perfect. I have to draw in a fortifying breath to resist, calling on reserves I've never needed before to extinguish the urge to kiss her. *I don't kiss.*

"Stay. I'm just going to get some supplies."

   THE DIRTY HEROES COLLECTION

I'm not sure if my tone conveys the erotic intent in my explanation, but she shivers all the same, and I get a rush of pure delight at the carnal smile that spreads warm and wanton across her face.

CHAPTER
Eight

THIS IS PROVING MORE OF CHALLENGE THAN I had anticipated. I have possibly the best equipped dungeon in the world at the club, but my home, since I never bring anyone here, is an entirely different story. Still, I'm nothing if not resourceful. I have raided the kitchen drawers, the cupboards, and the pantry for the last twenty minutes, much to Winston's amusement and confusion.

"What is it you are searching for specifically, sir? I might be able to point you in the right direction." He hovers at my shoulder, shadowing my every step.

"Nothing specific, Winston. I'm just searching." I pick up a long metal spatula from the utensil drawer and give it a cursory swish in the air. Satisfied, I place it on the tray next to the rest of my 'haul'. A frosting knife, hair brush, clothes pins, a peeling knife, a small ice bucket filled with cubes, a wine bottle, and from the equipment room, a length of climbing rope, some carabiners, and a rubber ball. I also have some not-so-subtle vegetables—a cucumber, carrot, and a rather large butternut squash, after all, everything's a dildo if you're brave enough. "Do we have any peppermint extract?"

"Is Sir planning on baking?" Winston arches his brow, his dry humor curling his lips.

"Funny. Do we have any?" I clip.

"We do," He walks into the pantry and returns with a small brown bottle of flavoring, places it on the tray, and continues to pretend he is not remotely interested in what I'm doing. He is, however, irritated that I'm doing it in *his* kitchen. Regardless, I shall be out of his hair shortly. I have no intention of divulging my plan. Even so, the wicked smile on my face is evidence enough that I am enjoying myself.

Tapping my fingers lightly on my lips, I muse to myself, trying to reconcile the plethora of desires I am eager to satiate with the tools at my disposal. It should be enough. I load the tray

     THE DIRTY HEROES COLLECTION

with a large bottle of water and take a bunch of the bananas from the table. Winston coughs up the sip of tea he had only partly swallowed.

"Food. These are for food." I explain. Lifting the tray, I catch the roll of his eyes and his tight lip. "And Winston…"

"Sir?" He faces me, impassive and resignedly obedient.

"I don't want to be disturbed. Understand?"

"Very good, sir. You know where I am if you need anything."

"I won't. I have everything I need right here."

"I'm very glad to hear it." He nods his head, and the warmth of his generous heart seeps out in the softness of his expression. I turn away before I say something kind and wholly out of character. I don't want to scare the poor man.

I take the supplies directly up to the bedroom, and while I can still hear splashing coming from the bathroom, I set about rigging up some vertical restraints, securing ropes to each of the corner posts to the canopy that is suspended above the bed. The canopy itself is sturdy enough to support a small car if it had to. One slight and sexy female form should be no problem. I lay out the instruments I gathered so they are close at hand and add a few more objects. A candle, some Vaseline, and two belts. I catch my reflection and can't believe what I'm seeing, a full-blown smile as wide as my face and only hint of my inner sadist glinting in my eyes. It would be unsettling if it didn't feel so completely fucking natural. I pull my shirt over my head and kick my joggers to the floor, opting for a lighter pair of briefs for the time being.

Heading down the stairs to the bathroom, I'm careful with my footsteps, avoiding the telltale groans from the ancient wooden floorboards, which would announce my arrival before I get the chance to spy on my guest. The sliver of a gap in the door is enough to peek through and watch. She's cupping handfuls of water, raising her arms high and laughing silently as she releases the water over her face, again and again. When she tires of this, she sinks down, disappearing for long seconds before bursting to the surface. She sweeps the hair from her eyes and runs her hands down the back of her head, neck, and down the front of her body.

It's decision time. Do I spy on her in the hope she's as curious to explore her tight little body as I am, or do I do the exploring? It's a no-

     THE DIRTY HEROES COLLECTION

brainer.

She jumps almost completely out of the bath, splashing back down with a nervous smile and a wicked flush to her cheeks as if she knows she was almost caught red handed.

"Good bath?" I ask. She nods.

"Are you ready to get out?" A more eager nod this time. I grab a large bath towel and she stands, climbing carefully over the high side. The towel swallows her up as I wrap it around her wet, naked, slightly goose pimpled body and shock myself when I don't immediately let go. In fact, I squeeze, pulling her hot little body firmly against mine. She sucks in a sharp breath and peers up. Her wet lashes look darker, and her eyes are so blue, I can see an endless ocean swirling in their depths.

"I have to tell you something, ask maybe, but either way, I have to explain what I want to do."

She's encased neck to toes in the towel, like a human sausage roll, completely at my mercy, yet the feelings surging inside are so foreign I'm not sure what to do next. Part of me wants to continue hugging her; part of me wants to whisk her away to my bed and fuck her brains out, and the more disconcerting part of me wants to cause her pain. Why is that disconcerting when it's how it's always lived my life? Well, I don't need to do it because it will ease my torment; my torment is already eased just being with her. This desire is rooted deeper. I feel the need for her pain and submission flow in me like my very essence. I know the pleasure will be immeasurable. I just know it. I've never had a problem with sadism, pain for kink, kink for kink's sake, I just never got off like others do. It was simply a process to fight the demons. But this, like everything with her, is different, and today is about discovering exactly *how* different.

I lift her up by her shoulders, her feet dangling. It's the least romantic way of carrying her I know; however, I think it sets the tone of what is about to come. I have already been uncharacteristically attentive, and before signals get mixed and misinterpreted, I need to set the record straight.

I carry her out of the bathroom and up the stairs. Her beaming smile is fucking adorable, and yet again, I feel her pull, like a powerful magnet, and I suddenly have iron filings running in my veins.

I sit her on the edge of my bed and resist the urge to drop to my haunches. Instead, I hold

                    THE DIRTY HEROES COLLECTION

my position, directly in front of her, towering and stiff in every sense of the word. Her eyes fix on mine, and she seems to understand the gravity of the situation. Her throat bobs with a slow swallow, and I catch her furtive glance at the straps hanging from the canopy frame above her.

I pick up my leather belt and run it slowly between my fingers. Looping it around her neck, I slip the end through the buckle and tighten. Her eyes flare with the first bite of leather against the tender skin on her neck.

"You like pain, and I want to explore that a little more. No, not a little. I want to explore that a great deal more." I tug the towel loose. Her skin is covered with gooseflesh, and I know it has nothing to do the room temperature. She squeezes her thighs together and drops her head back. I don't bother to remove the towel from the bed; we're going to need it later.

"You see, I inflict pain for a different kind of release, not for pleasure. You get pleasure, and I think, with you, I might experience the same." I take her hand and slip a loop over her wrist. I pull the rope tight, secure her wrists, and raise her arm high, out to the side. I repeat with the other hand, making sure the restraints are safe and not too tight. Any pain has to come from my expertise not my incompetence. I lift her waist high so she is now kneeling on the towel. I have to readjust the length of the restraints, and once I'm satisfied, I take a step back and admire the image before me.

Her arms stretched taut, biceps perfectly firm and curved, her ribs rise and fall with each steady breath, and her breasts swell and drop with each inhale, exhale. Her nipples are tight peaks of perfect pink flesh. I casually lean forward and suck one into my mouth, drawing the tip hard between my teeth. She bucks and leans forward to ease the tension but only as far as she can. I repeat the move on the other nipple, and before I release it, I hold the tender puckered flesh between my teeth and clip the clothespin I had palmed over the tip. Tweaking the other nipple, I clip the other clothespin in place and once more step back. She's sucking in deeper gulps of air, and her eyes are like inky wells with no visible color, only black desire.

I exhale, enjoying the sensations flooding my senses, alive where I have been barely living, lust where I have felt nothing, desire where I have been numb. I draw my thumb pensively

   THE DIRTY HEROES COLLECTION

across my bottom lip.

"I don't know if this is making any sense to you. I'm having a hard time coming to terms with it myself. It's just with you, I feel different."

I lurch forward, suddenly pained at the small distance. Snatching a handful of her damp hair in my fist, I yank her head back. She gapes in silent agony. Brushing my lips across her jaw, my breath washes her face. The words come out hoarse, a gravelly whisper filled with urgent need. "Everything about this, you being here now, feels different. It feels good. I feel… I… I…I'm not sure what to think. This test is as much for you as it is for me."

I bite down on the delectable area of skin she has willingly exposed for my pleasure. She shudders as I pull the blood in her capillaries to the surface of her skin, sucking with all my might. My marks on her skin, and I want them be good. I break the skin, a little, and the iron taste fills my mouth. She shivers, bucks and jolts, and when I release the contact, her eyes are glazed, and she is dazed and dizzy with desire. She drops her head to the other side, a clear invitation for more. My chest pounds with raw adrenaline, the power surging in my veins like a wildfire. I feel invincible.

"I want you to hold this." I place the small rubber ball in her hand. "If you need me to stop, since you can't speak, all you have to do is drop it; let it go, and I will stop immediately. If it's getting too intense and you just need a little break, squeeze it. It makes a sound, and I will give you a time out. Understand?" She squeezes the ball and grins when it squeaks like a cartoon mouse. She squeezes it a few times playfully, stopping when she faces me. This isn't *that* sort of playtime.

Picking up the Vaseline I scoop a small mound into the palm of my hand. I drop a few splashes of the peppermint extract and mix it in the greasy paste. I smear a pea-sized amount over the tip of her bright red, clamped nipple. She puffs out a shocked breath immediately, and I can only imagine the sting and tingles firing over that sensitive area. So cool it feels almost too hot, and then suddenly, its just too intense, and all one can do is absorb. I roll the remainder of the paste between my thumb and forefinger. Stepping closer, I hold it up to her nose so she can smell to cool, fresh aroma. Then, I take enormous pleasure in leisurely lowering my hand to her clit. She swallows thickly, and her stomach muscles tense when I press my thumb over her clit, making sure it's thoroughly covered. My touch might be enough to quell the assault of tingles, but I remove it too soon for her to garner any relief. She sags a little and then stiffens when I lean down and blow a blast of air over her core. Mint, cold air, and a little sensual intimacy is a good start, like setting a favorite dish to simmer on the stove. The longer it's left, the tastier it will be.

I wipe the Vaseline residue off my fingers and pick up the cucumber. I slide my other hand between her open legs, careful to avoid her clit. That has enough stimulation going on for the moment. Sinking two fingers inside answers that other niggling question: Is she going to need lube? She soaking, rolling her hips shamelessly, trying to get my fingers where she needs them. I pull my hand free and slap her breasts. She cries out with silent agony and shock contorting her face. I do it again.

"Your pleasure is mine. I give it.

Understand?" She nods, biting her lip flat, not quite quick enough to hide the nefarious quirk of a smile. Placing the cucumber at her entrance I ease it inside her. I've seen her take the candle; this is quite a bit bigger, and if I want to fuck her later, it's a good size for a warm-up. Feeling a little resistance, I push as far as I think is comfortable and then push a little bit farther until I see her toes begin to curl.

"Grip." I remove my hand, and the remaining few inches of the vegetable hang suspended between her legs. "Good girl, now I'm going to beat you, and if you let go of that cucumber I won't let you come. Understand?" She nods and shuffles to close her thighs. "No, keep them spread."

Her brow crinkles, and she worries her bottom lip. I grab her chin and raise it so her eyes meet my gaze.

"Just the beginning, angel." My words are softer, with an underlying encouraging tone that seems to instill some fire in her belly. She gives a firm nod and sucks in a steely breath.

I climb on the bed behind her, taking a strong position on my knees, arm's length from

   THE DIRTY HEROES COLLECTION

her naked back and perfect ass. I pick up the belt, and with my other hand, I stroke my finger down the length of her spine once and then can't help myself. I strike my palm hard across her ass cheek. There's nothing quite so beautiful as a palm print on flawless skin. She arches back, and I can see the cucumber drop, she instantly straightens and draws it back inside.

"God, you look glorious, and you are going to look so much more so when you are covered in welts. You have the ball; don't forget to use it." I swing my arm back and swipe it forward, the end it the belt strikes her hip, slashing a thick red line across her lower back.

I was right, glorious.

She drops her head back but keeps her body impressively steady as strike after strike, rains down on her skin. I feel like an artist gone mad with lust and a paintbrush. Marks of all lengths and varying depths crisscross her skin. I'm careful to avoid the kidney area; however, every other part of her is fair game. Her shoulders, her back, buttocks, thighs.

Lash after lash causes her to twist, contorting her lithe body within the constraints I have imposed. She's glowing, and I'm painfully hard.

By the time I'm finished, I'm breathless, delirious, and a little in love. The belt slips from my sweaty hand. I slide off the bed, take the bottle of water, and offer her a sip. Her breathing is shallow; her eyes are glazed, and her smile is fucking breathtaking.

She's fucking amazing.

She tenses when I reach between her legs, easing the cucumber out. It slips easily when she realizes I'm removing it and she no longer has to hold it there. She sighs, smiling with relief. I'm so impressed. I toss the vegetable, now glossy and slick with her arousal, on the bed. It must have been agony holding it in there. She motions for more water, and when she's finished, she juts her chin. It could be a challenging cue; however, the glint in her eyes makes me think she's just enjoying herself and wants some more.

Okay, then, let's step it up a level. I take the candle and light the wick. She grins. I know she's not afraid of a little wax play; however, in this instance, it's not the wax I need, it's the flame. I take the peeling knife from the tray. The blade is incredibly sharp and passing it through

     THE DIRTY HEROES COLLECTION

the flame, I can make it two things, sterile and hot. I blow the candle out and hold the blade between us.

"You have the ball?" I ask, my voice so gravelly I hardly recognize it. She squeaks the ball once. Her throat bobs and freezes mid swallow when I place the tip of the blade at her clavicle bone. Lightly dragging it down between her breasts. There's no cut, but the blade still leaves an instant red line from the heat. I reach the end of her ribs, and she's holding her breath. I tilt my head to one side. Her eyes lock on mine as I tilt the blade and draw my first line. The slice is small, not deep, and creates a burst of dark, glossy red liquid set to spill from the wound. Trickling in a single line toward her belly button, I bend close to quickly capture the first drop. My tongue sweeps up to the cut, wiping the wound clean, and when it fills again with her blood, I let it fall. I do this on the other side, small lines of agony that make her drip. Not blood. Pure arousal seeps from between her legs, so intoxicating, it's all I can smell.

All the plans in my head of torturing her to test myself, to see if this was real, evaporate with the overwhelming need to fuck, just fuck. I slash at the restraints; her arms flop to the side, and she collapses onto herself. Her wounds have already begun to close up, but I push her flat on her back to inspect my handiwork. She needs to be okay before I fuck her into next week. I use the edge of the towel and some water to wash the smears of blood. The darker streaks vanish, and when I wipe her skin dry, there's barely a mark on her. Her skin glows with fading welts and burns. I've never seen a canvas like it.

A deep groan rumbles in my chest when she whimpers at my soft touch when I cup and squeeze her breast. "Don't close your eyes." I reach back to the tray for the ice. She jumps at the first drop of freezing water that lands on her stomach. I trace the cube swiftly and lightly across her skin, leaving a thin trail of liquid along the edge of her hip bone, up her side, touching the curve of her collarbone, and down the valley between her breasts. Her skin prickles with the chill, and she trembles and gasps when I circle her nipples. I drop the cube in her belly button, and she bites back a squeal, her back arching slightly, and the muscles in her legs flex and tense.

I pick another cube and palm it, sliding it down her tummy and in between her legs. She jerks, opens her mouth with a silent cry, and her eyes scrunch tightly shut.

"Open your eyes." She tilts her head to look at me. I am now perched in between her legs. She pants, and tries to calm her riotous body with some steady breaths. She meets my imperious gaze with her searing one. "Cold?" I blow on her folds with warm breath but slide the cube over her glistening entrance.

She shivers, a visual confirmation of her plight.

"Would you like me to warm you up a little?" My warm breath kisses her core, and her hips tilt fruitlessly to try and edge closer to my mouth.

Her eager nod makes me smile, and I swipe my very warm tongue along the length of her silken, soaked folds. Her legs clamp around my head, an effective attempt to prevent the further onslaught of pleasure or perhaps maintain it. Either way, she slumps back in frustration when I quickly pull back.

"My way, angel. Understand?" Even to my ears, it sounds more like an order.

She gives a sharp nod and maintains my gaze. She smiles and her mouth forms a silent 'O' when I suddenly sink two fingers inside her. Her eyes are like saucers, and her little chest is frantic with rapid pants. I slowly pump, with a scissoring, twisting movement, and the heel of my hand rests with precision and perfect pressure on her clit. I rub gently while curling my fingers round and do the same to her sensitive inside. She bucks wildly when I hit her G-spot. Her whole body is a trembling erotic display of perfection. Her arousal is dripping onto the bed sheets, and I can't wait to bury myself inside her.

Just one more thing. I move my face close, kiss her inner thigh, and move slowly to where my fingers are working their magic. Each kiss closer to her core is a little harder; I suck the flesh a little deeper until I can feel her vibrating with erotic need. I draw in a

     THE DIRTY HEROES COLLECTION

heavenly breath, and I'm saturated by her sweet aroma. I bet she tastes like ambrosia. My fingers slide from her wetness, and I am on her like a starving man. I kiss, suck, and pull her tender folds into my mouth. I work my tongue like a viper, sweeping and licking every part of her. Her musk drives me like a rabid beast, and I can't get enough. I press my tongue flat against her clit, letting her hips roll against me. I'll give her this much. Her hand flies to my hair, and her thigh muscles lock around me. I can feel the tension in her frame as her orgasm begins to take hold. Her legs start to tremble, and when I push two fingers back inside and suck hard on her clit, she fucking detonates. Her body seizes, convulses and bows off the bed in a perfect arc. Warm liquid trickles from her, and I lap it up, nectar and musk. I can't get enough, and I can't wait a second longer.

I kneel between her spread legs. My rock hard erection in one hand, I lean over her and swipe my cock from her entrance to her clit, up and down several times. Her eyes fix me, pleading and fierce with lust. I sink inside in one thrust, and she cries out. Her silence is pained. Her muscles contract like crazy and take me completely by surprise. Her thighs flex and clench; her back curves, and her hands grip my hips like they are her lifeline. She comes hard around my cock, and it takes all my resolve not to follow her release. I pump gently inside, easing her down, her gasps turn to silent whimpers and inaudible sighs, her body limp and sated.

Rolling my hips, I continue to stroke into her, a gentler pace but ball-achingly deep. However, when languid becomes unbearable and my thrusts become more pounding, more urgent, more feral, I love the way she feels around me. I shift up the bed and rest my hands on either side of her shoulders. Her body undulates beneath me, grinding with me, meeting each thrust with erotic abandon. I stop before it's too late and pull out. I fist my cock and continue to pump hard. Our eyes train on the thick ribbon of come that shoots from me onto her tummy, the force splashing the edge of her breasts. I pitch onto one arm, and with my free hand, I smear my essence all over her skin. This is *my* way.

Closing my eyes, I roll onto my back, shaken, breathing heavily, sweat coating my skin. If I could form a rational thought, I would, but I'm too fucking high to process how fucking amazing I feel right now. How good she felt, how fucking perfect. Everything has shifted. I feel different. I feel happy. I feel alive. The bed shifts with movement, and opening my eyes, I have to laugh. This amazing creature that has me utterly bewitched is kneeling up next to me, an excited, expectant expression on her face, and her bright, piercing eyes are fixed on my still hard cock. What the hell? Why not?

"Be my guest."

I wave my hand in the general direction of my straining erection and watch it swell a little more when she bites her bottom lip.

She faces away with her back to me and raises her hips. She wraps her hand tightly around my thick girth and slips the head of my cock between her molten folds. She sinks down hard and throws her head back with a deep exhale. Twisting her head round, she flashes me a cheeky wink and starts to pump her tight little backside up and down my cock. Her back drops in a sensual curve as she leans forward, resting her hands on my legs above my knees. I could stare at this view forever. Soft round flesh bouncing and rippling with each impact drop against me, an erotic little grind against the base of my cock before she lifts herself almost free. My head is a mess, bombarded with the strength of feelings I've never allowed myself to experience before. I'm suddenly struggling to identify any of the benefits of *my way*.

She hovers for perilous seconds, which feel like agonizing hours because I know just how good it feels to be buried inside. Lucky for me she is in no hurry to deny herself. She drops down and repeats, increasing the pressure each time at the base of the journey and steadily increasing her pace.

I sit up so I am flush to her back, and her sweet little body glides against my chest as she moves. I slide one of my hands around and grab her breast, cup her neck with the other and twist her in my hand to meet my eager mouth. She sighs, her breath washes over me, and just before our lips touch, I throw my head back and yell.

"Fuck!" I moan, and the moment is gone, and I'm awash with a mix of loss and relief. It's too much, too soon. I can't. I'm not sure what I expect to see reflected in her eyes, but I'm more than happy with what I do see. Her lips are curled with pleasure, and her eyes shine with pure lust and fire. She wraps her hand around my balls, grips and tugs.

As fucking turned on as I am, as close as I am… She may control *where* I get to come, but she is not controlling *when* I get to come. I jerk my hips roughly, breaking her rhythm and making her grasp my thighs to keep her balance.

She looks nervously over her shoulder.

"My way," I remind her and watch her eyes, so dark and guarded, almost back and inscrutable. But her face is an unfathomable mix of nefarious confidence and vulnerability. "As you well know." My tone is a warning. I am under no illusion that she isn't fully aware of what she is doing. I push my hand flat between her shoulder blades forcing her more forward and onto her hands. I slap her glorious ass cheek with a playful strike and dig my fingers into her hips. I re-take control.

Loud slick sounds of skin colliding and desperate gasps fill the room. Her muscles grip me like a vise, scorching hot and coating my cock with her arousal. She feels like molten silk and takes me so fucking deep I want to die right here because I know this is heaven.

My hand slips between us, and I gather some of our wetness, slicking my fingers enough so that, when I press my thumb to her tight entrance it slips easily inside. I barely get my thumb inside to the knuckle when her muscles start to clamp down. I curl it round and stroke the thin layer between my thumb and my cock, which causes me to swell inside her just that little bit more. I didn't think that was possible. She crashes over the edge. No more breaths, no more movement, well, no external movement. Her body is taut and tense, silently riding wave after wave of euphoria. I feel each crest because her body saturates and spasms around my shaft. Shuddering, she draws in ragged breaths, coming down from her high as the pleasure ebbs. I pull her back onto me, hitting her deep inside and doing exactly what I had hoped.

She exhales, shudders from tip to toe. An audible cue but her sweet little center has already begun to grip, ripple, and contract around me. Fuck she feels so good. My hips jerk, and my jaw is clenched so tight I could crack a tooth. I thrust hard, hold tight, and chase my own release.

CHAPTER
Nine

GENTLY LIFTING THE SLENDER ARM DRAPED across my stomach, I find I have to force myself to move. I've never felt like this, at ease, happy, at peace, with an overflowing sense of fulfillment all at once, calming the tumultuous demons that have plagued my existence for as long as I can remember. Her beautiful features are soft and somehow ethereal as she rests in a deep sleep next to me. Her lips are only barely parted as she breathes, and the desire to kiss her wages a fierce war inside me. If I had a moment to really think, if I was being honest with myself, I'm not sure why it's a battle at all. What's stopping me? With every fiber of my being, this feels right, so why don't I trust this is real? Why is there still a seed of doubt when every fucking thing about her is perfect? Everything about the last two days has been fucking perfect. I said it last night, and I feel it in my damaged soul: This is *heaven*.

Fuck doubt and fuck the curse; it was broken the moment she saved me. I know it. The moment I was dragged from that car, I felt different. I didn't know it was because of *her* and now I do.

She exhales softly. Her smile is impish, her lips tipped only at one corner, and she seems to be dancing somewhere between a deep slumber and a dream state, which has her writhing and undulating her sweet body enough to make my cock twitch. Fuck after last night and yesterday, I'm raw. I'm not complaining, but if she is half as sore as I am, I think today is going to be needed for some serious R & R.

My legs feel like lead weights as I drop them over the edge of the bed and endeavor to slip out unnoticed. My body seems more reluctant than my mind to leave her, and it's an effort to drag my ass away and put on some clothes. Catching my reflection in the mirror, it's not hard to guess the cause of this reluctance. Sheer exhaustion aside, I have a huge smile spread

   THE DIRTY HEROES COLLECTION

across my face, so natural I didn't even feel it, only the image staring back at me makes me take stock. I don't think I've ever seen that level of joy on my face, honest and unashamed. Yeah, fuck exhaustion, it's her; she's done this. *She's the one.* I slip my jogging pants on, and barefoot, I silently descend the stairs from the master bedroom to go in search of sustenance.

"Good morning, sir." Winston folds his newspaper and stands as I enter the kitchen. He's sporting the same knowing grin he's had since I brought my guest into the house. If it was at all possible for *anything* to irritate me in my current good mood, I'm sure his smugness would be wearing a little thin by now; however, *nothing* is going to do that, not a damn thing.

"Good morning, Winston. I'm starving." I rub my stomach as if he can't hear it growling as I walk closer. I take the paper he set aside and flip it open to check the headlines.

"Why are you reading last week's paper?"

"I haven't finished the crossword," he replies drolly, removing the paper from the table before I can annoy him further and offer to finish the crossword for him.

"Would Sir like some poached eggs and salmon?"

"Sir would like that very much, thank you." Perching on the edge of the kitchen table, I notice that there's no music, no radio. Winston always has the radio on for company. I walk over to the side and switch the retro radio on. It crackles to life.

"And the young lady?" he asks as I fruitlessly try and find a station.

"Is this broken?" I give it a shake, because that is my level of technical expertise when it comes to electronics.

"And the young lady?" Winston repeats, irritation clipping his tone. I replace the radio, deciding it's clearly not an issue for him. I give it no more thought and answer his question with a wry smile.

"Is still unconscious. I'll take something up after I've checked my messages. Speaking of which, have you seen my phone?"

"It's on the side there, by the bread bin. I took the liberty of removing it from your bedroom suite." He points his gnarled finger to the oak dresser by the back door.

"I'd say that was more than a liberty, Winston. What the hell!" I snatch the phone from the side and swipe the screen. The hairs on my neck prickle with agitation. I refuse to get angry. I refuse to let anything kill my buzz. Nevertheless, I feel a fiery glare is justified.

"You said you didn't want to be disturbed," he explains.

"I've got thirty missed calls, Winston." I scroll the screen.

"You seemed to be enjoying yourself, sir. I didn't want to interrupt you unless it was an emergency." The dismissive tone would normally send me over the edge; however, the deep sense of calm I have prevents any such outburst.

"And thirty calls didn't seem like an emergency?" Sarcasm isn't anger and is also justified.

"Thirty calls from Miss Stephanie, regarding work no doubt, so no, I didn't consider them more important than your happiness," he states categorically, and any aggravation evaporates. I *have* been happy.

"I appreciate that; however, she is not going to be happy with you." I sniff and raise a warning eyebrow. He scoffs and begins the breakfast preparations.

"Let me add that to the list of cares I could not give."

"I'll tell her that." He shrugs, the lack of

concern rolling off his shoulders as he beats the eggs in the bowl. I press the return call button on my phone and motion for Winston to bring my breakfast into the study as I walk backwards down the hall. Stephanie picks up on the second ring.

"Where the hell have you been?" Her voice is pitched high, anxious mixed with excitement.

"Busy."

"Well, you are going to want to bring your ass back to the club." She sounds like she's grinning from ear to ear with glee.

"And why is that?" I reach my study and push the door open. The room smells of dying embers and warm whiskey.

"Because she's here," she blurts, giddy, and I get a sick feeling in my stomach. Stephanie is never giddy.

"Who's there?"

"The girl, the woman, more like. The one that rescued you. She's real!"

"What?" I stop in the center of the room as if her words have flooded my veins with ice water, freezing me to the spot. I've become an ice statue.

"I said, she's real," she repeats. Her excitement is clear as she continues to bombard me with information. I'm numb. "She showed up last night. She's a doctor or something, saw your car go over and like some sort of super hero, she dived in after you."

"What?"

"Look, I know you can hear me, Eric, get your ass back here and see for yourself." She sniffs, a short sound accompanied with an incredulous sounding chuckle. I'm hollow. I don't understand. The numb void is suddenly filled with too many questions.

"How did she find me? Why didn't she stay with me after she dragged me out? Where did she go? Why now? I don't understand." The last statement is an echo of the confusion messing up my head and dominating every coherent thought my fucked up brain is trying to conjure.

"How about you come back and ask her for yourself," Stephanie quips.

"She can speak?"

"Yes, of course she can. I mean I haven't asked her to sing or anything, but I can guess she's got a killer voice, all salty and sexy as hell. Eric, she's a Siren, absolutely stunning. You were right all along. And now, I don't understand, why aren't I hearing engines revving?"

"I don't...I..." I choke on my own doubt.

Sweat gathers at my temples, and my heart is racing so fast it feels like it's about to explode in my chest.

"This is what you wanted, Eric. You said she eased your demons. Didn't she?"

"Yes, but—" I can't finish my sentence. I look up to the heavens, hoping for some Devine enlightenment. What do I do? I close my eyelids, and all I can see is the woman asleep in my bed, my perfect angel and yet…

"But?" Stephanie interrupts my inner turmoil.

"But nothing. I'm on my way." It's simple. I have to know for sure. I stride from my study, every step hastening my pace, and in no time I'm at my bedroom door. Silently, I steal into the room, gather my shoes, a T-shirt, a sweater, my wallet and my keys. I'm jogging by the time I reach the front door. Winston appears from the kitchen, carrying a tray of delicious smelling breakfast food.

"Sir?" He tilts his head with confusion.

"I have to go." My vague explanation sounds like an apology to my own ears.

"Might I ask where?" His calm tone belies the worry in his heavy brow.

"I have to see for myself. I'm sorry Winston,

 THE DIRTY HEROES COLLECTION

please give the breakfast to…" My gaze flits to the upstairs, and I have to shake myself. The pull to go to her is almost unbearable. I'm in utter conflict. Torn between truth and my own desires, it's like a blade slowly slicing into my heart to see if I will bleed. I am bleeding, yet I know I will never be settled, never truly find peace if I don't see for myself. "Stephanie said she's real," is the only explanation I can manage to mutter to my confused employee.

"Oh, I don't think you needed Stephanie to tell you that, sir." His misunderstanding is accompanied with a warm accommodating smile. His gaze follows to where mine had just been, but when he looks back to me I have to drop my eyes to the floor. When I look up again it takes everything I have to meet his gaze.

"No, not her," I state flatly. "The woman that saved me. She's real and she's in the city. I have to go to her. I'm sorry." I step outside and falter. My chest feels tight, the pain knotting so much it hurts to breathe. I know this pain. It's familiar and constant. That call has burst the fantasy bubble as sure as an arrow through soft flesh might cause a fatal wound. This wasn't real; it was a fantasy.

How could it be anything other than a

dream? It can't, not if one phone call can so quickly and completely plummet me back into darkness. I felt the light briefly. It warmed my face and warmed my soul. It was heaven, but heaven isn't real for men like me. I need to see the woman who saved me. I need to know where the fantasy ends and the truth begins. I need to see for myself if she's the one. And even if she isn't, seeing her will do one good thing. It will prove I'm not insane.

The tires screech on the gravel, sending plumes of grit and dirt high in to the air in the wake of my speeding car. I glance in the rearview mirror and wish I hadn't. In the window above Winston, a desolate figure in an oversized t-shirt is banging against the glass. I don't look back again.

The tension in the tendons in my leg throbs and aches from the constant pressure I've had pressed on the gas for the last few hours. I haven't stopped, haven't answered my phone, haven't even listened to the radio for fear of being distracted. All I can see in my tunnel vision is killing me from the inside. Every time I blink, I hope to see the vision that saved me that night, and all I can see is the angel I left broken in the

     THE DIRTY HEROES COLLECTION

window of my castle. I've never second-guessed myself. Good, bad or indifferent I am always certain of everything I do, yet I have never felt this level of anguish before. Like a dripping tap, I have to constantly remind myself: *That* is the *only* reason I'm driving a hundred and twenty on the freeway, speeding toward the city, for answers, for certainty, for truth.

The traffic usually gets heavier as I reach the outskirts, the urban areas becoming more dense with tall buildings and people, but today, it's eerily quiet. Slowing to a crawl, I take the opportunity to check my phone. I've had several missed calls from Winston, which I expected, and none from Stephanie, which I find odd, considering the last conversation ended with me heading out the door. I would have thought, at the very least, she would've checked on my progress. The thought is gone from my head the moment it enters, replaced by the rotating images of the woman who saved me and the one I left behind. By the time I pull up outside the club, my addled brain can't distinguish between the two, and it feels like the morphed image has been burned onto my retinas.

I lock the car and swipe myself into the private entrance at the rear of the warehouse. If one didn't know the club was here, one would never notice it. It's the best kept secret in the city for a reason. My members want their kink like I want my personal life, *private*.

It's early afternoon. It's taken longer than I thought to get here, and now that I am, I'm impatient as a bull in a china shop to get my answers. I tear through the darkened corridor toward my office. It's empty. I spin on my heel and barge my way into the main bar and mingle room. Since the club doesn't really liven up until midnight, I'm surprised there are any members at all; however, there are a few gathered around the bar and in booths dotted around the staging area. I walk over to the bar.

"Where's Stephanie?" I snap at the server I don't recognize.

"She's with a her sub in playroom B." The nervous barmaid looks over to her supervisor, someone else new I assume since I can't put a name to the face. The barmaid is unsure if she's said the right thing. I don't have time to set her straight. No, she hasn't said the right thing, but fuck it, I'm the motherfucking boss, and if she didn't answer me, the mood I'm in, she'd be lucky to just be collecting her things at the end of her shift.

	

Pushing off of the bar, I stride across the main room toward the back rooms, dungeons, and playroom B. I don't knock, and crashing the door wide open, I don't even bother glancing through the modesty panel. Stephanie has her arm pulled back high and loaded with a cat o' nine tails. Her bare assed sub is bent and tied over the spanking bench. Stephanie spins at the sound of the door, her face like thunder, lightning, and a little of the fires of hell in her scowl.

"What the fuck, Eric? You don't just barge into a scene uninvited," she spits, fury coating every word.

"I *was* invited. *You* invited me, well, not to the scene, but back to the club, now where is she?"

"Where's who?" Her hands are on her hips, the whip still held tight in her white knuckled grip, anger mixed with confusion. Anger is winning, and if I wasn't so wholly pre-occupied, I might feel bad at pissing her off quite so much.

"Not the fucking time for games, Stephanie," I growl

"Really? Because this is a playroom and you've just barged in—"

I bark my interruption. "Stephanie!" Her

lips snap tight, eyes wide as waves of fury roll off me and surge toward her. Grinding my jaw, I clench and unsuccessfully force myself to tone the anger down a notch. "I swear to god, tell me where she is."

"Eric, I don't know what you're talking about."

"The woman, the woman who saved me is here. You called, you told me she was here. You told me to come and see for myself." Each word of explanation seems to bounce off her as if these are the ravings of a mad man. Only *this* mad man is also someone she clearly pities.

"Eric, I didn't call. I wouldn't. Not when you're having a break." Her soothing tone feels like a rough abrasion on raw nerves.

"You didn't call? But I spoke to you." I mutter. A swirl of nausea threatens, and I have to swallow down the acrid taste forming at the back of my throat. I feel dizzy, dazed. I think I'm swaying on my feet. I can't focus, ground myself. Is anything real anymore?

"Eric, I didn't call. I've been in scenes all day. Well, this morning I was doing the shopping but I am hardly likely to call you with that riveting information. Eric? Eric, are you all right?" Stephanie reaches for me, a comforting hand

     THE DIRTY HEROES COLLECTION

that seems to burn my skin when she touches my hand. I snatch mine away, out of her reach. I don't deserve her kindness.

"What have I done?" I buckle with the sheer weight of pain punching me in the gut.

"Eric, you're scaring me."

I stumble from the room, dazed and ricocheting off of the narrow corridor walls as I try and make my way to fresh air. The eerie luminous green of the fire exit sign glows, guiding my way out of this hell. My vision blurs, and nausea rolls in my empty stomach. Bursting through the door, I collapse to my knees, retching only saliva and air from my hollow stomach. I can't breathe. My skin feels itchy, cold, like a sickness is coating it, suffocating me from the outside.

"What have I done?" I call out to no one, howling to the empty sky as panic claws at my raw nerve endings. Sucking in large gulps of air, it feels like I can never get quite take in enough to quell the panic, to feed my oxygen-starved brain.

Think Eric! Think!

I reach in my pocket for my phone and speed dial Winston. It rings and rings and rings. I don't dial again. I'm on my feet, racing back to my car. This time it's Stephanie in my rear view mirror, looking distraught. The angry roar of the V12 engine is thankfully drowning out the turmoil in my head that threatens to unhinge the tentative grasp I have on this fucked-up situation. What grasp? I have no grasp. I fucked up, I was tricked, just as I felt the first a slither of happiness, *real* happiness this…*this happens*. Well, I won't let it ruin me. I won't let it drag me back to the darkness. I found my light. I just have to get back in time to tell her, to *show* her.

My phone buzzes beside me and the hands-free system in the car kicks in.

"Winston, is she there? Tell me she's still there." I can hear the desperation in my voice. My fingers grip tighter on the wheel, and my foot pushes harder on the gas.

"Yes and no."

"Really not the time to be cryptic." My low growl weights my comment with a threatening tone.

"She is no longer *in* the castle. She's standing on the bridge. Has been there since you left, sir. I tried to get her to come back in side."

"The bridge?"

"Yes, exactly where the barrier is broken, where your car tore through and plummeted into the ocean. You know the place."

"I am familiar, yes." I briefly close my eyes at the ridiculous remark and my equally flip response. "You have to get her back in the castle."

"I tried sir. She won't budge. Every time I tried to get close, she stepped right to the edge. I was afraid she'd fall if I grabbed for her, and my reflexes aren't what they once were." The remorse in his voice is genuine. I can almost picture the old man's frail grip faltering, and as much as I can't forgive myself for putting her in that situation, I see no need to drag him into the mire with me.

"Fuck!" Slamming my fist on the center of the steering wheel, the car horn screams out to no one. A few moments pass, and drawing in a steady breath, I am able to calm my thoughts enough to speak again.

"Have you tried talking to her?"

"I have, sir."

"You need to tell her I'm sorry. Tell her I'm on my way back. Tell her…" My throat closes up, choking the words to an inaudible whisper.

"Yes?" Winston urges

"Tell her not to fucking jump."

"I may have mentioned that bit already, sir. She just holds up three fingers and looks over the horizon at the fading sun. She did that the first night, I just don't know what she means."

"It means she dies, Winston. It means she dies in three days." I hear him gasp. The blade that has been slicing into my chest since I learned of this cruel deception digs a little deeper.

"It's only been two. You still have a day, sir."

I scoff at his optimistic tone. "You think? Because funnily enough, Winston, I'm not getting that impression, what with her standing on a bridge staring down at the bottomless ocean."

"But she doesn't know you're coming back, I'll go and tell her now." I hear the positive conviction in his voice and allow myself a fraction of that hope to lift my spirits.

"Yes, do that. I'll be as quick as I can."

"Do you want to speak to her?"

"I want that more than anything, but you know there's no signal outside of the courtyard.

Just go to her, stay with her, and for fuck sake, don't let her jump." The call ends, and I'm left with the silence in the car and the storm inside my head. It's the last place on earth I want to be.

CHAPTER
Ten

PURE FEAR AND ADRENALINE ARE THE ONLY things keeping me functioning enough to drive this car. I'm thrumming with excess energy and undiluted terror coursing through my veins like a toxin. I haven't had to stop for fuel; my usually thirsty car seems to be running on air. I'm not complaining. I'm grateful I haven't had to waste time stopping. The endurance of driving such a distance pretty much nonstop should have me in tatters. My bloodstream should be crying out for an overdose of caffeine and sugar. Yet I've barely taken a sip of my bottled of water, and I can't stomach the idea of food even though I know I should be famished.

The car roars at the foot of the valley, and

I swing the beast around the corners like it's on rails, skidding on the lightly used winding country road that leads to my castle. One more mountain to traverse and I'll be home, *safe*. My heart is pounding so hard it feels like it's going to crack my ribs. Sweat trickles at my temples, and my hands feel like rigor has set in already; I haven't shifted their position in over eighty miles. The rear of the car fishtails as I swerve, and trying to right it, I miss the iron girder anchoring the bridge to the mainland.

In the distance, I can see her. The white of my t-shirt flutters against her fragile frame. She sways slightly, and as the last few rays of light cling to the horizon, there is a golden glow like a halo of light all around her. She looks like an angel, *my angel*. I floor the gas and cover the distance in no time. I leap from the car, and she's in my arms before I've had the chance to let go of the breath I seem to have been holding since I left the city.

"You, it's *you*. I'm sorry. I'm so sorry." I'm holding her face in my hands; tears fall like rivers from her aquamarine eyes. She sucks in gulps of air while holding my ardent gaze as she holds my once cold heart in her hands. I may be saving her from whatever the fuck she was about to do, but she's saved me, *twice*. My lips crash to hers. My tongue dives in to her sweetness. Her tongue twines round mine, dances, duels, and leaves me breathless when we part.

"Oh, Eric." She gasps, the sweetest sound, only she looks so sad, desolate and heartbroken.

"Am I too late?" I capture her face in my hands, pleading eyes searching her face for forgiveness. *She has to forgive me.* She smiles, a tender sweet curve of her lips. Her soft fingers trace the frown lines on my forehead and flutter down the side of my face, along my jawline. She presses her forefinger over my lips.

"You were too late the moment you left the castle," she says, her voice a hypnotic melody that belies the words she's saying. *No!* I start to shake my head. She removes her finger, tips up on her toes, and moves her face close to mine. Her eyes, filled with sorrow, shine with unshed tears, the sorrow masked momentarily by a flash of sweet pain, making her pupils darken. Her breath washes over me, intoxicating. Her lips feel like nirvana pressed to mine. I'm suddenly light as air, floating high, entwined in her arms, enraptured by her spirit, and enthralled by the soul shattering kiss.

I'm flying, soaring, falling, plummeting, sinking into darkness.

It's so cold.

I'm frozen, chilled ice for bones. Stricken with terror, my eyelids spring open. It takes a fraction of a second to orient myself. I wasn't floating. I wasn't even falling. I was crashing. The steering wheel has exploded into a white powdery bag. Cool blood trickles from my nose, and darkness surrounds the windows as the swell of water rushes to fill the space created by the car hitting the surface of the ocean. Like invisible hands, eddies and a strong current pull the vehicle down into the depths. I fight to release the seatbelt. It clicks free. The front of the car dips into a sharp dive, as if being dragged by an overly eager sea monster. I've seen the movies, I know how this works, I have to let the car fill with water before I can open the door and escape.

The electrics fade as water begins to pour in through gaps and cracks in the car's chassis. I kick my shoes off, and loosen anything that might hinder my escape. The rising water fills the footwells, quickly gaining ground until the icy ocean filling the car is making it hard to breathe. There's a tightness in my lungs, and panic tears through me as I realize I won't have time to escape. The temperature is too severe. My basic motor functions will begin to shut down before the car fills enough to open the door. The temperature paralyzes my muscles. Even if my fingers do cooperate enough to grasp the door handle, I don't have the strength to push the door open. The water is pressing like an anvil on my chest. The headlights fail, and I'm plunged into complete darkness. I have no idea how deep the car has sunk. I know I won't get out this time, and then it hits me, harder than a head-on collision and just as fatal. A revelation, the ultimate cruelty I will suffer for all eternity.

My time at the castle with her felt like heaven, because it *was* heaven. There is no *this time*. I should never have left the castle, because I never made it out of the car, last time.

THE END

SNEAK PEEK

The Masked Prince

CHAPTER ONE
Alex

My stomach growls, and I swear I hear it echo off the bricks of this dark alley. The small piece of bread I scavenged from the dumpster behind the bakery earlier in the day has long since become calories burned. I don't have time to scrounge for more food; I need to pick a mark and claim a bounty before the inn is full for the night.

I scan and dismiss near a dozen possibilities before catching sight of the man in the elegant suit and tall top hat. Rings adorn his fingers and an expensive-looking pocket watch dangles carelessly from his coat. It's the kind of job that will guarantee room and food for a week.

I wait until the man passes the mouth of the

alley, then I step right into him. I quickly snatch the watch, shoving it into the pocket of my loose slacks. Grabbing his arm, I pretend to steady myself and mutter apologies. My hand slides down his coat sleeve and along the fingers of his left hand, rolling two rings into my palm.

"So sorry, sir," I say and hurry away down another alley.

I make it to Joe's pawn with seconds to spare. I toss my new wares onto the counter and wait. Joe's is filthy and under better circumstances I wouldn't be caught dead here. But beggars can't be choosers and all that. We all pay our dues at some point, I guess now is my time.

The items Joe buys and sells are for the most part illegally obtained, and he doesn't bother keeping up pretenses with cleaning and maintenance for the few honest citizens lucky enough to walk through his doors. Most items are repurchased by their owners for an exorbitant amount within a day or two anyway, so there's no need for him to pretend he's selling. The glass display cases showcase common pawn items: cheap rings and musical instruments. All covered in a layer of dirt and dust.

"I'll give you two fifty, kid."

"What? The rings are worth a lot more than two fifty themselves. Including the watch, it should be at least a thousand."

"Whatever, boy. Two fifty. Take it or leave it."

I consider the benefits of taking the lowball offer versus convincing Joe to give me what they're worth. Before I can tell Joe my decision, the bell at the front door rings a warning of an approaching customer. Most likely another thief come to collect his earnings for the night.

"I'll take it."

Joe hands me some crumpled bills, and I hurry back out to the streets. Two fifty won't last as long as I planned. I'll need to make some more cash soon, but for the night I'm well off, as long as I can make it to the inn before they're full.

I run down familiar alleys, taking every short cut I know. The Sultan's Consort rents the cheapest rooms in town, by the night and by the hour. It's almost midnight, which means if the street walkers haven't already rented a room, they'll be flocking to the inn to secure one for their next client, or clients.

I reach the wooden doors to see them closed and locked. A sign declaring no vacancy hanging from a rusted hook above the frame.

Upset at my circumstances, I kick at the door before slamming a fist into the hard wood of the door. The sound of laughter reaches my ears, deep and sultry. Spinning toward the sound, I see the shadow of a man at the corner of the building near the alleyway.

"What's so funny?" I snarl the words.

"I'm sorry. But your tantrum was rather comical." His voice is as rich as his laughter.

"Well, I'm glad my misfortune can provide you some entertainment for the night." The sarcasm in my words is unmistakable. The man takes a step forward into the streetlight before quickly stepping back.

"I may have a solution to your problem. A long-term solution."

I'm not sure what he thinks my problem is, but anything that will get me off the streets tonight is something I'm willing to hear. "Go on."

"I'm in need of someone with your talents. I

am looking to acquire a rather valuable artifact, and I'm willing to pay handsomely for your help."

He wants me to steal something for him? Sounds too easy.

"You want me to steal something? That's it?"

"Yes. Tomorrow."

I knew it. "Yeah, well, I need something tonight. Catch me tomorrow and I may be interested."

I turn away, prepared to find an empty alley where I can rest for the night.

"One thousand dollars." He shouts at my back.

"What?" I look back at him over my shoulders.

"I'll give you one thousand dollars for the night."

"And what would you want in return?"

The man finally steps into the light. He is handsome in a dark and sinister way. His black hair is slicked back, and his brows arch in a villainous tableau. His body, which hints at being tone and fit, is covered in clothes much too elegant for the likes of the streets in front of The Sultan's Consort. But it's his smile that sends a shiver of warning through me. Whatever he wants from me tonight won't be anything good.

"Nothing much my dear boy, just the pleasure of your body."

"I'm not a whore." I may be a thief, but I've never sold my body. I've had countless offers from both men and women, and I've considered a few, but sex is an intimate act, one I won't sully with greed.

"You mistake my words. The thousand is to secure your services in the morning. The pleasure of your body will be a bonus because we both want it."

I don't trust he's telling the truth, but the promise of a bed and money destroys my resolve. "Okay, but I don't want you and I don't think I'll change my mind before the sun comes up."

"Challenge accepted."

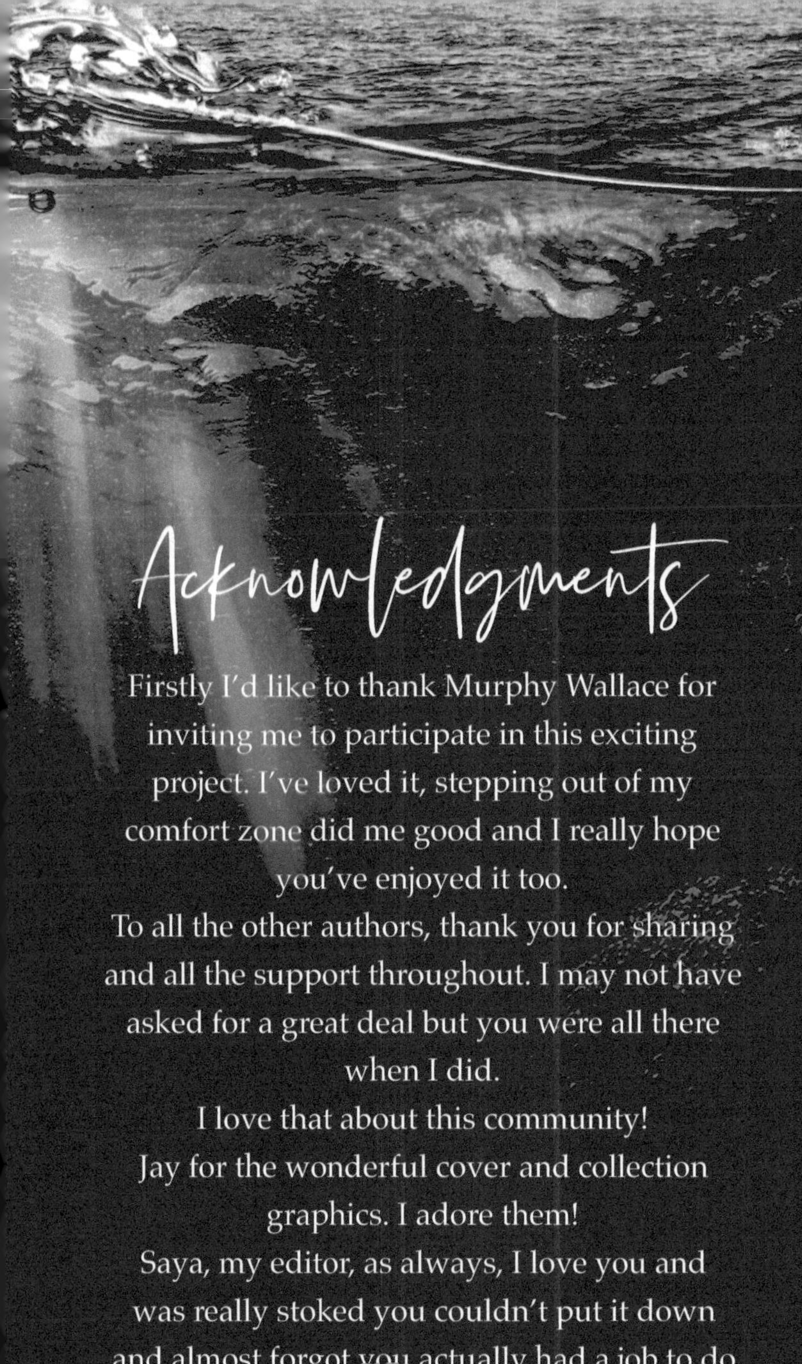

Acknowledgments

Firstly I'd like to thank Murphy Wallace for inviting me to participate in this exciting project. I've loved it, stepping out of my comfort zone did me good and I really hope you've enjoyed it too.

To all the other authors, thank you for sharing and all the support throughout. I may not have asked for a great deal but you were all there when I did.

I love that about this community!

Jay for the wonderful cover and collection graphics. I adore them!

Saya, my editor, as always, I love you and was really stoked you couldn't put it down and almost forgot you actually had a job to do.

while reading it.
Dani René for formatting, love it!
My street team, Alison, Jami, Caroline and
Sarah, as always I'm so thankful for all you do,
no matter how small you think your input is, it
is *greatly* appreciated.
Shannon…I have no words babe, you're my
little star and rock!! Love you sister.
And you, my lovely readers, I'm thankful
every day that I have you and
am gobsmacked that you like what I do…
THANK YOU!
Oh,
And PLEASE leave a review!!!!

For other books by Dee Palmer
https://deepalmerwriter.com/

For a FREE novella
https://dashboard.bookfunnel.com/
books/101702/giveaways/2954057426577398

SNEAK PEEK

Disgrace

Buy Link

https://www.amazon.com/dp/B01FOIRIYI

PROLOGUE
Sam

Sixteen Months Ago

"You still there, Sam?" I can hear the concern in his voice, but it fades into the mix of nerves and sickness threatening to escape my mouth. Saliva pools at the back of my throat and I swallow, the slight metallic taste an indication that I have scraped my teeth against some soft tissue. My jaw is clenched so tight I didn't even feel the bite. "Sam!" His tone is urgent almost panicked.

"I'm here…sorry. This is harder than I thought it would be that's all." I grip the phone a little tighter, angry that my hand is actually trembling.

"Look, wait there. I can be there in an hour. You shouldn't do this on your own. I told you this but you never bloody listen." He lets out an angry breath, which makes me smile. All my life I never had someone care about me the way he does. I am so very grateful. I tell him often enough, but it's never enough. He saved me.

"No…no don't come, Leon. I will be fine. It's just a house." I swallow that pooling water again. So loud this time I can hear him let out a sigh filled with only a fraction of the sadness welling in me.

"Yeah…just a house. Like Manson was just a guy. Sam you don't have to do this in person. The solicitor can deal with this shit. Come home. You can beat the crap out of me and make us both feel better."

I bark out a dirty laugh. I love that he can turn my mood on a dime. "God, I love you." I feel some tension leave my frame when I push out a fortifying breath. "I will be fine. I am made of much stronger stuff…now." I add before he reminds me of the empty, broken girl he slowly helped transform ten years ago.

"Call me when you're done…and the offer

still stands." His silence is filled with hope.

"Leon, I found you an excellent replacement and you need to start using her." My tone is resolute if a little sharp.

"I know…I know…It's just when you've had the best—" His flattery will get him nowhere… absolutely nowhere.

"You're my best friend, Leon." I add softly.

"Which might be an issue if we were fucking." He is pushing me and I feel all that tension back.

"Leon!" I snap. "Enough…You can be such an arsehole!"

"But you love me?" I can almost see the devilish grin creeping across his dark features. We share similar colouring, rich coffee skin, deep brown eyes and impossibly dark brown hair that falls just shy of jet black.

"I do." My tone is clipped.

"Did it work?" He asks after a short silence and before I get to ask what, he adds. "Are you feeling all angry and distracted now?" I sniff out a laugh and shake my head though he can't see that part.

"Yes, Leon…Thank you." A tentative smile

tips the corners of my lips, sleek and shiny with my trademark red.

"My work here is done. Now go and sort the house of horrors…and come home. Where you belong." He hangs up and I chuckle. He never says goodbye.

I straighten my shoulders and hold on to the false bravado trickling through my veins hoping it's enough to get me through this next hour.

It's a beautiful cottage. The perfect picture of an idyllic Home County village dwelling. Honey coloured, washed out stone, four tiny windows under a mottled, red slate roof and an old oak front door with polished wrought iron fixings that wouldn't look out of place on a church. The Old Rectory, my family home. The garden is bare now, cut back and pruned to within an inch of its life. My mother would spend hours—days—tending the flower beds. She craved the attention it brought from passersby, strangers, people who meant nothing.

The bones of the wisteria cling to the front of the house like some distorted exoskeleton, the branches so thick the blooms would block the sunlight from the windows in the spring. I slide my key into the lock. She didn't change the lock when I left. Why would she? There was no need, I was the one who left, and I promised I'd never return as long as she lived.

The door opens to a shrill discord of creaking hinges loudly objecting my presence. I push the heavy door wide with a firm shove. The stale, dry air hits me with an aroma brimming with memories. I puff the air from my nose. I have no desire to reminisce; memory lane is for masochists. There is only one room I want to see.

It's been so long, but I need to remember so I don't let it happen again. I walk through the dim hall, lit only by the soft winter sun spilling in from the open front door. Everything is neat and tidy with a fine layer of dust that only now dares to settle. Now she's dead that is. I drag my finger along the welcome table, swirling patterns, irregular and petty. Her coat is still hanging from the gnarled hatstand, and I wipe the dust from my finger on the thick woollen sleeve.

The stairs exhale a painful groan with each

step, and I find myself hovering on the final tread. This was the only step that made a sound when I'd lived here. This was my warning. I place my foot down and feel my tummy tighten as the unique sound makes my foot start to shake. I stamp it down heavily. The sound is different this time, and I stamp my other foot, too. *No need to fucking tremble, Sam. She's not here,* I reprimand myself. I stride the remainder of the corridor and don't hesitate when I reach for the door handle of my old room. I step inside.

I'm surprised. I don't know why I'm surprised, but I thought she would've changed it. The small metal framed bed with the pink floral covers and a rickety bedside table with no lamp. The walls are plain light grey, as are the curtains cinched back with a thick rope tie. Above the bed and on each wall hang several embroidered pictures. A different prayer for each of my sins. My lips thin with bittersweet amusement. The walls would collapse under the weight of prayers needed for my sins now. I look to my feet just inside the threshold.

"There…something that has changed. That is new," I say to myself. The point on my toe all shiny, in patent black knee high lace up boot, flips the corner of the new rug which is awkwardly placed at an angle by the door. "And that is why." My voice catches, my eyes clamp tight and my hand flies to my mouth, an attempt to stop the sob that's being wrenched from my chest. *Don't you fucking cry one more fucking tear in this house.* I dig my long acrylic nails into my palms with such force the pain is exactly enough to stop my tears. I turn and walk to the window. I need some air. I lift the window catch from its cradle and push the small lead-encased pane, but the window is jammed. I roll my eyes. It's not jammed; it's nailed shut.

I let out a sharp laugh that bounces uncomfortably around the still silent room. It's funny how, with time, your memory tries to trick you. You rewrite your own history. Some memories are exaggerated to make them a little more intense or a little more amusing. Others are suppressed, and some you think couldn't possibly be as bad as you remember, so you do yourself a favour and forget. I shouldn't have come.

"Hello!" A gruff voice calls from inside the

house. "Hello, Ms Cartwright! Is that you?"

"Upstairs," I reply and take a steadying breath. I hear Mr Brown, the solicitor in charge of my mother's estate, climb the stairs and I watch him stumble and trip into the room. Flustered he tries to compose himself. He kicks the badly placed rug exposing more of the bare floorboards.

"Who places a rug there, like that?" He pulls the cuffs of his jacket one at a time to straighten the bunched up material. "Oh…Look at that." He muses and leans to take a closer look. "I can see why now but still…it seems a stupid place." He mutters, "What do you suppose that stain is?" He tips his head at the mark but my eyes are already fixed in the shadow on the wood… my mind unfortunately is hurtling into my past.

"Blood…lots and lots of blood." I don't recognise the chill in my own voice, and Mr Brown turns to look at me as if for the first time. He doesn't respond to my macabre declaration. Well, he might have, but I don't hear him. As much as I fight it, the flashback hits me like the first strike of a palm across my cheek, and I recoil as I stand just as I did back then.

Sam aged seventeen

"You filthy little slut!" His voice is menacingly low and he draws his hand back to strike me again.

"Richard, please!" I cry holding the heat in my cheek from his hand. It doesn't hurt. I've had worse from him. Even his words don't slice me like they used to, but the fury today distorts his face. Harsh lines twisted into an ugly scowl, thin lips pursed and pulled tight into a hate-filled grimace. He doesn't look like my boyfriend. He looks like a monster. Clenching his fist this time, he swings and cracks my jaw so hard I feel it like a blade behind my eyes. An unbelievable pain that knocks me to my knees.

"You spread your legs for me quick enough. How do I know the little bastard is mine, hmm?" He sneers at me, down his too straight nose, his blue eyes wild with anger, spit now dripping from his lips.

"Richard, please. I'm sorry. It's was an accident. That one time maybe, when you…you didn't wear the condom." His eyes widen, and I shrink rushing quickly to rectify my mistake. It's too late he hauls me up by grabbing a fistful of my hair and throws me against the wall like a rag doll. Strange, I never thought him to be that strong, with his slight build. But he is taller than me, and obviously, with the pure hatred running through his veins, his strength is no match for me. "Richard, I didn't mean it was your fault. You know my mother…I can't risk taking birth control. She would kill me if she knew what we'd done." I plead into vacant eyes.

He strides over to me and again grabs my hair, my scalp tender from hairs being torn from their roots. I grab his forearms to try and support my weight.

"Yes…let's not forget your social-climbing mother in all this. She really believed me when I said I was going to marry you. Christ! To think I would have someone like her in **my** family…someone like **you**. A half-bred slut, who's probably fucked every boy in the village while I was at boarding school," he mocks.

"Richard, don't…that's not true. I love you." My voice is horse from crying, and I choke back the words when his large hand reaches around my neck.

"Say that again… whore!" He squeezes and I gasp for air. His eyes darken, and I feel him harden against my stomach. Jesus, how can he get off on my terror? The thin cotton dress is no barrier at all. I panic because this doesn't feel like the times he has abused me in the past. Something has changed in him. He looks unhinged. He needs to calm down or he's going to really hurt me. I soften my voice.

"Richard, my love, of course I love you. There is only you…you **know** that." I struggle to swallow against his grip. He loosens a little, and I let out a breath and try to smile. It catches when I realise, too late and with utter horror, his intention. He pulls his arm right back and levels a punch directly into my stomach. I collapse gasping for air that won't come, winded and in agony I roll onto the floor. My arms wrap tight across my tummy trying to protect what's inside.

I flash a glance at the monster before me just in time to see him let his heavily weighted boot swing forward. Easily crashing through my arms, again and again. Pounding his full force and weight into my abdomen. I try to curl in on myself tighter, but he grabs my head and stretches me out. I limply take punch after punch to my face. The pain is everywhere but the only noise I can distinguish is his heavy breathing and the sound of softly crunching tissue and sometimes bone. I can't seem to scream…cry…I *can't find my voice at all.*

"Who makes you happy, sweetheart?" His demonic chant rings in my ears. He always asks the same damn question, every time he hurts me the most. He repeats but emphasises each word this time with a carefully placed brutal kick to my stomach. "Who. Makes. You. Happy. Sweetheart."

I try to answer because I know from experience he won't stop until I do. But large floaty black spots seep across my glazed vision, tempting me into the darkness when an almighty cramp shocks me enough to sit bolt upright. Richard steps back and we both look at the large dark mass of liquid running between my legs. My white dress quickly unable to absorb any more of the blood as it drips, drips onto the floor.

"Richard, please." I cry and hold my hand for him to help. The confusion in his face must mirror mine. Why won't he help me? Can't he see what's happening? Can't he see I need help? Can't he see I'm going to lose the baby?

"It looks like we're about done here, don't you think?" He pulls his cuffs down and brushes at the specks of my blood that now pepper his sleeves. Little streaks and smears cover the pristine white material. "What's good for getting blood out of cotton?" He

inspects the material like it is the only thing remotely significant. I'm haemorrhaging badly, and the agony is barely masking my utter devastation. I drag myself toward the door just as it opens. My mother steps into the room and gasps. Not because she has seen me or the blood, but because having Richard in my room is strictly forbidden.

"Mr Brookes-Hamilton, I know you intend to marry my daughter, but please do not take liberties with my kind nature." She gushes with her false reprimand, but her colour drains when he pushes the door a little wider to reveal me in a crumbled heap, losing more blood than I can spare.

"Mother…please." I manage to cry before I sink back into myself.

"Oh, Grace, what have you done?" Her grave words are laced with accusation and venom. "Mr Brookes—"she pleads as Richard moves to her side. "—Richard please don't go. I am sure there is a very good explanation." She reaches for his arm to stop him from leaving but his thunderous scowl prevents her actually making contact.

"Oh, there is, Mrs Cartwright, there is…Your daughter is a whore." I hear her suck in a sharp breath as his footsteps recede quickly or maybe my level of consciousness fails to distinguish the sound of him walking away and he is still there. I don't care anymore, I just need help.

"Mother, please, you need to call an ambulance." I reach for a hand that isn't offered and freeze when I recognise that expression of stone and hatred settle on her implacable face. Her beady blue eyes narrow and her cheeks burn with anger. She looks like she is desperate to once more spew all her hatred and bile. But not today it seems. I know that everything bad that has ever happened in her life is **my** fault. She's drilled it into me since I could talk, and now I have just ruined her chance at a life she believes she deserves.

My hand falls to the floor, skidding in the sticky mess and I slump down, flat on the boards. I manage to turn my head and meet her gaze…She could freeze ice with the warmth of her compassion for me. She's not going to help my baby…she's not going to help me. She steps back through the door and leaves me in an ever-increasing circle of my own blood. She leaves my baby to die and I don't doubt for a moment she hopes I will too. I pass out to the sound of a solid click of the door closing and the turn of the iron lock.

"Miss, are you all right? You don't seem to have heard what I just said." I feel the cold chill as the sweat from the flashback that instantly coated my skin, just as quickly dries. I shake my head even if the residual image is too fresh to ignore. My heart is still racing, but I hold my arm out as steadily as I can.

Mr Brown is a portly man, and that is being kind. He is most likely in his early sixties with thinning grey hair and tiny, wire-rimmed glasses. His beady eyes comically widen when he really sees me for the first time. I get this a lot. Even living in a cosmopolitan, vibrant city like London I know I stand out, but in a sleepy village such as this, I must look like an extra from Underworld in a Miss Marple Sunday afternoon special. My choice of wardrobe was very deliberate today, though. It's my armour. I offer my hand, and I swear he bends as if to kiss the back of it. I raise a brow and he stiffens with embarrassment. He shouldn't be embarrassed; under any other circumstance it would be charming. In certain situations it would be expected. He opts now for a light shake and I offer him a warm smile.

"Grace Cartwright, I presume." He is slightly breathless and I think there might be a little drool on his chin. I pull my hand sharply from his hold and straighten my back. His expression flashes from gentil to guarded.

"I legally changed my name when I was eighteen, Mr Brown. I'm Sam Bonfleur. I took my grandfather's surname." I correct.

"And Sam?" He nods but starts leafing through the pages of papers he has clutched to his chest.

"After a drink." I gave it no more thought at the time other than I didn't want to be called Grace ever again.

He chuckles as if I were joking. I wasn't.

His sudden frown causes more deep-set wrinkles to form. "I'm glad you could come today. Your mother had many antique pieces I am sure you will—"

"Sell everything. I want nothing. Honestly, I didn't think she would've kept me in her will at all." I keep my tone level and, with considerable effort, maintain a much softer timbre than I feel. Rage and sorrow blend and course through me; my nerves are raw and knots the size of footballs roll in my stomach. Mr Brown shifts uncomfortably and won't meet my eye.

"Um yes…you are right. Sadly, I believe that was her intention." He clears his throat. "There was some irregularity in the documentation and essential forms weren't completed correctly. In such cases the will is nullified and by default the estate would be bequeathed to the *closest* living relative." I scoff derisively at his misplaced assumption and inwardly smile that my mother would be turning in her grave at this outcome.

"Only *living* relative." I correct and draw in a steadying breath. Did I honestly think she would've softened over time and this be her final gesture of forgiveness? Of course not, she was evil, and evil is timeless. I shake myself free of the useless thoughts. "Regardless, it is what it is. You have my instructions. I just came today…" My voice catches, he doesn't need to know why I came. He doesn't need to know my gory past. "Sell it all." I repeat.

He looks a little shocked but nods. "I know it's of little comfort, but you will be a very rich woman, Ms Bonfleur." His smile falters on his pallid face, and there is sweat beading on his top lip. I make him uncomfortable. I smile. I like making men uncomfortable.

"I am a very rich woman already. I don't want a penny from the sale. I don't want to take anything for a keepsake. It is all to go to the charity I listed. You have something for me to sign?" I hold my hand out expectantly.

"Why did you come then? We could've done this over the phone or at my offices." His tone is a little irritated when he hands me a small stack of papers with little markers. I quickly work my way through signing my childhood away.

"I needed to remind myself. I needed this fresh in my mind so I won't do it again." I curse myself that I mutter this out loud enough for him to hear. I return his pen and he nods with kind eyes of understanding.

"Fall in love." He offers with a knowing look but my bitter laugh cuts him dead and now I do feel like I have to clarify…He does need to know.

"Not fall no, sometimes that sadly can't be helped. But I needed to remind myself why I will never again tell someone I love them. All men lie, Mr Brown, but once you tell a man you love him, he seems to think it gives him certain rights, rights to hurt and control you." I take my time to look him up and down, my glare accusatory. I feel only a tinge of shame that I judge all men by the one very bad apple, especially when I know it isn't true. Leon isn't like that, but it is better to be safe, to live by this rule than die being sorry. "Never again will I let someone control me." I step past him but turn when he coughs for my attention.

"Sorry, Ms Bonfleur, but I need a forwarding address. I can't use the PO Box I'm afraid, but perhaps I could send it to your office," he stutters.

"My office?" I hold back a smile.

"I noticed you had passed the bar. I assumed you were practising law somewhere?" He is checking his notes again, and I let out a light laugh.

"You have been busy." I turn to face him, drawing up to my full five foot ten height, six foot in my heels. His cheeks pink and he drags a finger across his shirt collar. He has the decency to look a little sheepish.

"You took some finding." He shrugs and

I bite my lip. He obviously didn't look hard enough or he wouldn't be asking this question. Or maybe he did.

"I qualified but I don't practice, Mr Brown." I raise my brow and fix him with a glare to see if he withers…To see if he is hiding my secrets and trying to play me but he doesn't flinch. Satisfied he knows no more than he has alluded to already, I hand him my card, my smile widening with the stretch of his upturned brow. "Send whatever you need here. This is where I work."

"What do you do?" He flips the black card over. There is nothing on the back and just my signature on the front and the club address.

"I'm a whore." I smile sweetly at his sudden dropped jaw.

It's not until the houses start to crowd together, vying for prime location space that I start to relax. The endless expanse of lush green fields diminish to tiny pockets of manufactured parks and protected communal areas as the train speeds closer into the heart of the city, toward my home. My *real* home. Leon was right. I didn't have to be there in person to sort the sale. Documents could easily be signed and witnessed elsewhere but something made me want to remember. No, not something… *someone*. Jason Sinclair.

Despite what *I* call myself, I don't fuck for money. I fuck because I want to fuck, and I wanted to fuck Jason…very much. A hook-up with a hot guy at Bethany and Daniel's. That was *all* it was supposed to be. I knew his reputation for absolute dominance. He's a silent partner in the club I work for, for Chrissakes, but I felt safe to cross the line in a civilian setting. I could blame the whole 'weddings make people crazy' notion but… well, I might've mentioned Jason Sinclair is fucking hot! Taller than me by several inches but eye level when I'm sporting my six-inch killer heels, broad, built shoulders that narrow to perfection in his immaculate three piece navy suit. Light brown hair with natural flecks of gold that just beg to be gripped and tousled. But his eyes, oh God, his eyes. As if the rich honey with the same golden highlights hypnotically swirling wouldn't captivate a mere mortal. The intensity with which he wields his most potent weapon, well I was a fool to think hooking up was anything but his decision.

A one-time thing, I could handle a one-time thing. It is all I have ever done since leaving home. Not so many as to warrant my moniker but always just a one-time thing. I can feel the hairs on my neck dance as a delicious chill sweeps my body when I recall the moment when he put his strong palm around my neck and squeezed a little too tight. I came so hard I couldn't breathe. I wanted it…I wanted more, but more shocking still, I realised I wanted him, and that thought terrified me.

That is why I didn't return his calls and that is why I came today. I needed to remind myself why I won't let another man control me…ever.